WHEN DESTINY CALLS

WHEN DESTINY CALLS

CAROL SMALL

When Destiny Calls

Dedication

To Julia and Roberta, special friends - precious gems in God's showcase.

To Caroline another dear friend and her beautiful girls - Carissa, Evangeline, Annalisa and Lily.

CONTENTS

Prologue

Welcome, this story – an allegory based on The Song of Solomon, has been written with you in mind. Your destiny. The specific, noteworthy purpose for *your* life – you could view it as the path you are called to take, your special assignment and its fulfilment. This is locked up inside you at birth and unveiled as you journey through life. If you take the roads afforded and intended for you, your appointed outcome will be achieved.

So let's take a look at a young woman who dreams of destiny and how she attains it. As you read about her - answering and eventually completing the course she is called to take, fighting fears, gaining courage and standing for truth, think about your own course.

Is it a result of fate or faith? The odds are not against you when you truly believe *your life matters*. If you listen deep inside you - the voice of conscience, the good desires of your heart and the call of your Maker will all direct you to *your* destined place.

1

A Timely Visit
"I sleep, but my heart is awake"[1]

The wind howled as it rustled the boughs of the aged weeping willows outside. Grey clouds brooded over the city of Lincoln, threatening a heavy downpour. The Georgian antique bracket clock located on the marble mantelpiece chimed seven times on this late-summer Saturday morning. Uniformed postmen and postwomen were on their allotted rounds; newspapers were being delivered.

As the two coincided at the welcoming bungalow home of Mrs. Hopkins, a curious conversation followed at her front door. Their departure left Mrs. Hopkins with a knitted brow and pursed lips as she held on to one of the white porch pillars, looked up at the darkened heavens and then returned behind closed doors.

Lily awoke with a start, her nightclothes wet with perspiration; her heart beating wildly. She had experienced yet another nightmare, the images of the day before were haunting her, stalking her weary mind. She had tossed and turned all night trying to snatch a few moments of rest.

She could still hear the anguished cry of her friend Charity as they pulled Jim to the riverbank. Jim's face was constantly before her, his distorted, lifeless expression. Just moments before, he was happy and light-hearted as ever. Despite her frantic attempts to resuscitate him, Jim never regained consciousness.

At times it seemed like a bad dream that wouldn't go away, but it was more than that. Having spent the remainder of the evening with Charity at the Central Police Station, giving her statement, confirming the worst to Jim's parents and receiving counselling and comfort, she knew that this was real. Terribly real.

Nevertheless, it still seemed beyond belief. Jim was dead. *Dead!* Their world had been rocked. She had chosen to go home rather than sleep over at Charity's. Both women were distraught and stricken with grief.

Jim Preston had been like a brother to them, the brother neither one of them had. He was a handsome, active, strong, carefree kind of guy who loved to show off his brawn, his benevolence and his brains. He had won numerous trophies in sporting events, his favourite being swimming. That's what made it so bizarre. How could *he* drown, and so quickly? He was even a volunteer lifeguard, yet in his hour of need his knowledge could not save him. Neither could Charity nor Lily.

They had spent the afternoon celebrating their examination results and their acceptance into the universities of their choice. Jim liberally poured the champagne. He toasted their mutual success with his usual banter. It was obvious that they all had too much to drink. None of them was prepared to be sober, to be watchful and so their pleasure trip turned into a panic-stricken scramble for life.

While they were all frolicking, Jim had stood up and leaned over the rowing boat, thrusting his weight in careless abandon, destabilising the vessel. Prior to that moment Charity had called him crackers and he had taken off his designer trainers and offered them as blue cheese. The next thing they knew was the cold water stinging their faces as their world went topsy-turvy. For a moment it seemed funny, but the air had then changed and Jim's laughter was silenced. The current was pulling them along and the capsized boat was in its tow.

Lily fearfully called out Jim's name as she felt for his body. Where *was* he? The water was deep, but Jim was used to that. Charity thought for a brief moment that he was up to his usual antics, but instinctively knew something was wrong. Lily felt Jim's shoulders by her knees and yelled to Charity to help her raise him up.

Both women fought the current and their fear to pull him ashore. As they did so, Charity desperately cried out to Jim to pull through. Lily quickly retrieved Jim's mobile phone from his front, buttoned, left pocket. Fortunately his was housed in a waterproof case. She punched in 999 and found her voice to request immediate help. The dispatcher spoke with Charity while they awaited the paramedics.

On the bank of the river Witham, it was clear that Charity's cries had fallen on unhearing ears. Jim was not responding. Her attempts to revive him using first aid techniques proved futile. She closed his eyelids with trembling hands, then cupped her hands to her face and looked at Lily as tears streaked from her eyes. Lily was shivering, too choked to speak, her mouth twisted with grief and her eyes opened wide with shock.

Jim lay cold, silent and barefoot in his soaked striped T-shirt and blue denim shorts. His tinted blue sunglasses as well as their brown ones were in the river. Lily's loose multicoloured sandals were absent, Charity's tan leather ones were buckled and sodden as were the rest of their clothes. They appeared to be in a trance. It seemed just then that nothing was moving, but the river and that they were in a hopelessly deserted spot.

Ten minutes later, the two girls rode in stunned silence as the ambulance took them to LCH, the county's local hospital.

♡ ♡ ♡

This morning, Lily pulled the ivory, Egyptian cotton bed sheets over her and convulsed in deep groans. Memories of her parents' death two years ago, flooded her anguished mind. The phone rang suddenly, startling her out of her distress. It was now twenty minutes past ten.

The voicemail indicator was still flashing and Lily realised that she had accidentally switched on the auto button when she hit the snooze button at ten o'clock. Reluctantly, she reached over and picked up the receiver.

"Lily, it's Mrs. Hopkins," but Lily interrupted her caller.

"Look I just really need some peace and quiet to think and..." Lily then broke down in tears.

Mrs. Hopkins, her former history teacher who had also taught Jim, insisted that Lily allow her to come around. At quarter past eleven, Mrs. Hopkins entered the cosy flat where Lily lived on her own. A 'Do not Disturb' sign was hung on the door outside to make Lily's neighbours aware of her need for solitude, as was her custom during her preparations for exams.

Still dressed in her nightwear and pastel green terry robe, Lily welcomed her friend's comforting embrace and then hung her navy blue storm jacket and umbrella on the coat stand. In her hand, Mrs. Hopkins carried an eco-friendly shopping bag which she set down on the wooden floor.

"Miserable weather, isn't it?" Mrs. Hopkins declared while straightening her clothes.

She wore a white jumper with dark grey trousers and white leather loafers. She smoothed her short, dark brown curls while looking in the oval mirror hanging in the hallway.

"Suits my mood," replied Lily in a dreary tone.

They both settled down on the ruby-red plush three-seater sofa in the lounge. The coloured venetian blinds were still closed as Lily wanted to shut out the world in her pain. She had managed to prepare tea for Mrs. Hopkins' coming and had helped herself to a cup. Mrs. Hopkins joined her, pouring the steaming brew into the china cup on the glass coffee table. There were open photo albums and the high school year book at the far end of the table.

Having previously learnt that Lily was an only child and orphaned by the tragic death of her parents Mr. and Mrs. White in a plane crash, Mrs. Hopkins had taken it upon herself to be a friend and advisor to Lily. Shirley Hopkins was a tall, trim, single, middle-aged woman who had never married or had any children. This however had freed her to give time and substance to care for the various people who crossed her path.

The memory of her parents' death was again gnawing at Lily's soul as she vainly tried to suppress it. She had shouldered the blame for having persuaded her mother and father to go on a cruise to the Galapagos Islands for their holiday that year. They never returned - their excursion flight from Santa Cruz Island to Guayaquil crashed with no survivors.

Lily had been hospitalised with trauma, in denial for a fortnight. Mrs. Hopkins had stayed with her and organised a support system comprising mainly of friends, neighbours and teachers.

There was no extended family to assist. Her mother had no siblings and her dad had lost his two brothers in military combat. Lily's grandparents had died many years ago in New Zealand. It was decided that a memorial service be held when Lily was strong enough to attend it. Lily refused to stay at the family home and moved into Manor Views, where she could begin her life anew.

"I wish I hadn't booked the trip to Italy," Mrs. Hopkins said to Lily apologetically.

"O, but you longed to go, it's an expedition of a lifetime, an adventure for you really," Lily replied, momentarily forgetting her troubles. "Please don't let me get in the way of you enjoying yourself and fulfilling your dreams. Life must go on you know." She paused then added wearily, "...for some of us at least."

"Yes it does, but I'm very concerned about how you'll cope in the next few days and weeks, my dear."

"I... I'll make it through somehow." Lily's eyes brimmed with tears as she bit her lower lip and continued, "I just can't believe Jim's gone."

Mrs. Hopkins put a comforting arm around Lily as she gave way to her grief. After a few minutes, Lily raised her head and pulled some of the tissues out of the square box on the coffee table and wiped her eyes and nose.

"It's so uncanny that he should die in water. He was born in water you know. It was his element you could say. He planned our day out on the river six months ago." Lily stopped talking and just held her face in her hands.

Breaking the awkward silence, Mrs. Hopkins commented, "Jim was an exceptional student and likeable young man. He'll be missed by many."

She then retrieved a newspaper from the shopping bag and said to Lily, "When you feel up to it Lily, you may want to read the wonderful tributes to Jim mentioned in today's paper."

Lily lifted her head once more and took the newspaper with a heavy heart. On the cover page of *The Lincoln Herald* was a picture of Jim Preston, taken from his school photos. It was a look she had often seen before, his jet black, curly hair nicely combed. He wore a broad smile, his light green eyes twinkled with mischief. He had such hopes, such promise. He was a handsome lad with a beckoning future, too young to die, Lily thought to herself.

He intended to major in Physical Education at Columbia University. All of that was now history. *History!* It was in that class they had met and struck up a good friendship that included - Charity and yes, Mrs. Hopkins.

Inside the paper was a picture of herself and Charity. Charity Scarlett sported an alluring smile, her blonde, straight, shoulder length hair and olive complexion offset her sky-blue eyes. She was a stunning picture of beauty and ambition.

Lily had a fairer complexion, grey eyes and medium brown, long, wavy hair that was pulled back off her face. Her expression was more serious with a faint smile on her lips. Charity and Jim were eighteen years old, while Lily had just turned nineteen.

"It doesn't seem fair," she eventually said to Mrs. Hopkins. "How come we survived and he didn't?"

"Life is that way, the unexpected can happen or does for the most part, history reveals that," Mrs. Hopkins replied.

The expression on her face was understanding and kind, just as her voice. Lily looked into her ocean green eyes with wonder at the circumstances that had brought this precious, caring woman into her life. Yes, she'd rather be with her parents, but they were not alive - she would have to settle for Mrs. Hopkins. Then who? People seemed to be drifting out of her life. Lily glanced at a framed picture of her parents on the wall.

"A service will be held at Holy Cross I'm sure, but I won't be here for that, as I leave tomorrow. If it wouldn't cause contractual problems, I'd opt out right now," Mrs. Hopkins wistfully remarked.

"No, Mrs. Hopkins," Lily responded, "you can't go back on your promise.

You committed yourself to this archaeological project. It would only add to my grief if you abandoned it. You have already done a lot for me, for which I'm truly grateful. I'm glad you came by today. Just talking with you has helped me open up to deal with the shock of it all."

After they had conversed for a while, Mrs. Hopkins noticed a glimmer of a smile on Lily's face. It meant so much to be a friend in times of need and to help brighten the heart of a loved one. Mrs. Hopkins reached into the shopping bag lying on the oak floor and said, "I've brought you a Bible, Lily. I know you objected to taking one in the past, but I believe that I must give you this as a present and a good source of help in my absence. Please take it and read it sometime, will you?" Mrs. Hopkins' whole being seemed to plead with Lily.

"All right, I'll take it because you're my friend, but I don't care for religion much, as you know, and I can't grasp the concept of God with all the pain and heartache I've encountered. My parents never believed in Him."

Taking Lily's free hand into hers, Mrs. Hopkins replied, "The truth is Lily, you are somewhat closer to Him now, for He is near to those who are broken-hearted and is a present help in time of trouble."[2]

"Where was He yesterday then?" Lily remonstrated. "I'm not blaming God okay, but why should I believe He's going to help me now, when He didn't help me then? And where was He when my parents were in need?" Lily retorted with rising indignation.

"Lily," Mrs. Hopkins said softly, aiming to placate and not upset her grieving friend, "let me explain a little about my knowledge of God. He is a caring, loving Father. He longs for us to know Him for who He really is. He meets us where we are when we are willing to trust Him in spite of our problems," Mrs. Hopkins paused, covering Lily's hand with her other palm.

With a gentle smile she carried on, "God promises to work everything for the good of those who love Him.[3] He desires a relationship with each one of us Lily, as I've shared before - one based on His unconditional love and trust. One based on His faithfulness and sacrifice. His love for you is greater than the pain you've experienced in life. If you choose to open your heart to Him, He will fill it with the reality of His love."

Lily vaguely remembered what she was hearing. Mrs. Hopkins had indeed spoken on these matters before and Lily politely accommodated her then, while purposely tuning out the words. Now it was going in one ear and lodging on the surface of somewhere.

Taking another item from the shopping bag, she continued, "I've also brought an inspirational CD with soothing songs of encouragement on there, feel free to listen. It's another gift. I've used it in my own time of special need. I love you Lily and want you to be in the best hands, okay?"

"Okay," Lily said slowly, "Thanks for your thoughtfulness. I know you truly care"

"Are you hungry?" Mrs. Hopkins asked.

"Not much, really," Lily answered shaking her head.

"Would you like me to fix you something? I've come prepared, you know," she said with a smile.

"Go ahead, but keep it small - I don't have much of an appetite. You do the kitchen thing while I dress and check my messages."

Mrs. Hopkins was a culinary master in her own right. She would create and gather recipes from her trips and contacts and was always on the lookout for a cookout. She indeed was one who cared for the whole person - spirit, soul and body.

Wearing a black cotton T-shirt and matching jeans, Lily came out of the bathroom to find the coffee table spread with tasty, fragrant morsels - finger-licking dainties which were quite irresistible. This was her first meal since the tragedy. They both sat down to savour the treats and talk some more. After the meal, Mrs. Hopkins agreed to Lily's request to help her pack for the trip.

Hours later, as Lily got out of Mrs. Hopkins' silver Lexus, she stated, "If there is a God and He is good as you say, then I expect you will come back."

Mrs. Hopkins squeezed her hand gently. "I know one person who has promised He will. Goodbye Lily."

They waved goodbye to each other as Mrs. Hopkins reversed and drove off. Lily looked up at the overcast sky and after picking up the flowers and cards left by her door, entered her flat, feeling very lonely and uncertain about her future.

2

Friendship Matters
"What is your beloved more than another?" [4]

The funeral was a stressful time for Lily. She stayed with Charity for the weekend. To be alone would be wholly unbearable. They took a special trip out of town to shop for new mobile phones and something appropriate to wear. Lily had thrown out the black dress that she had worn to her parents' memorial service. She had grown in many ways since then. As they browsed in a trendy boutique Charity solemnly declared, "We must look our very best for Jim."

"Absolutely!" Lily stated as she flicked her wavy hair back and held a dress on its hanger close to her shoulders while she viewed her image in the mirror.

Both girls were very fashion-conscious and considered shopping as a lifetime hobby. Even while jogging together their kit was nothing but classy, their make-up waterproof and appealing. They decided on above-the-knee length dresses with no sleeves, black lace gloves, sling back pumps and purses. Lured by the pungent aroma of coffee beans, they stopped for lunch at Cello's.

"Don't you just love this place?" Lily commented trying to be a bit light-hearted.

"It's second to none," Charity replied as she settled on the leather bench and stared out of the window.

"*Fait accompli.* Aren't you forgetting something?" Lily asked with a slight smile.

"Oh yes, the menu," Charity agreed and then let out a huge sigh unable to shake the huge ache and sadness in her heart. After a quick scan both girls decided on the triple-melt, coffee sundae.

"Do you remember when Jim stepped in between you and George?" Charity reminisced.

"Do I ever! It was right over *there.*" Lily motioned with her head.

George Pickering, had interrupted Lily while she was paying for her order and brashly tried to smother her with kisses in an act of bravado in front of his mates. Lily tried to push him away, grabbing his face and stepping on his feet with her high heeled pumps. He had yelped in pain and disbelief.

"I'm forever grateful Jim intervened. What a... prat! How did I *ever* think of having a relationship with *him*?" Lily responded shaking her head in disdain.

"Don't ask!" Charity replied with a wide smile, as she picked up her purse and they went to freshen up.

Next they visited Jim's favourite hangout, the Sport Zone, where they collected a distinctive plaque to be mounted in his honour. As Charity got behind the wheel of her red Micra, she couldn't help shaking her head and saying, "What is man, when he can be so strong and yet - so weak?"

♡ ♡ ♡

On the dreaded, dismal day they rode together to the church with a wreath in hand. Charity's parents were in the front of the car, as they made the silent journey. The weather however, was pleasant. It was warm, with a light breeze and few clouds. No rain was forecast. Charity and Lily were asked to sit with Jim's family at the front of the building. Jim's body was laid in a cedar casket.

There were two large wreaths already on the top, one of yellow roses from the school, the other of blue carnations, eucalyptus and pine cones from the family. Charity laid the red carnation and white lily wreath beside them, then joined Jim's relatives. Lily found the service a very moving and heart-rending experience. There were many people in attendance. Jim was certainly popular. The church was filled to capacity. A large framed photo of Jim stood on a circular table beside the casket.

Mr. Dean a tall, slim, erudite gentleman, the principal of Lincoln High, read the eulogy while peering over his oblong spectacles. His thin, silver hair was rapidly receding unlike his sharp memory that grew year upon year. The Heads of the PE and Science departments, as well as some of Jim's team members, shared their best memories. Charity had agreed to give a special tribute to Jim. She struggled to release her words, expressing the heavy yoke of sorrow on her soul.

Lily wept through the speech, as did other students, friends and relations. Mrs. Preston kept blowing her nose; her tears cascaded down her cheeks and her hands as she leaned against her husband. She wore a broad-rimmed, black hat covering her short, blonde hair and a tailored black skirt-suit with white piping and black pumps.

Jim's dad fought tears throughout the service. He was totally dressed in black - his shirt, tie, suit and shoes all matched his hair. His sad, dark-brown eyes were fixed on the coffin. Lily was thinking how deeply it must hurt them to lose their only son.

The minister, Reverend Watson, was warm and lively in nature. As if in response to Lily's unspoken concern, he said, "God also intimately knows the pain involved in the death of a loved one; He too was separated from His only Son." Lily's attention was now keenly focused towards the minister.

He seemed to be talking straight to their hearts, urging all to be prepared to meet God whether they lived a few years or many. He, like Mrs. Hopkins, spoke of God as a friend and his soft, blue eyes seemed to gaze lovingly at their souls, yearning for all attending to be certain of their future. He spoke of walking with God each day and the joy of knowing Him, being able to converse confidently and constantly with Him.

"To be close to the One who created us for Himself, because He takes pleasure in us."[5]

Lily had never thought that God, whoever He was, would be pleased with her.

"To know Him is to welcome death when it comes as a doorway into His eternal presence,"[6] the minister said.

She didn't recall hearing any such thing at her parents' memorial service. Then again, she had been miles away in thought and grief. This minister however, made death seem hopeful instead of dreadful. The hunger in her heart for deep companionship drove her to listen in earnest.

"The way to know God is through Jesus Christ, the One who died and rose again, who took our judgement so that we could receive His mercy.[7] He took our filthy rags of sin, so we could have His regal, right standing with God. It's the state of your heart God looks at, not your appearance."[8]

It was the last thing the minister said in his message that pierced her heart deeper.

"Knowing Jesus Christ as Saviour and Lord, greatly affects and improves your quality and enjoyment of life now and in eternity."[9]

When the invitation was given, Lily fought the impulse to respond as she felt it would distract from the focus on Jim. No one raised their hands. Somehow, her broken heart was melting.

Jim was to be buried on the grounds of Holy Cross Church. A sombre procession flowed out of the building to the burial plot. Charity and Lily held each other as they moved along, wiping their eyes. Guilt still clutched their hearts, trying to keep them hostage to their regrets.

If Jim had been romantically involved, this might not have happened, Charity reasoned. Then again, it could have been two funerals instead of one. Did Jim plan to die? She quickly dismissed the thought. The endless possibilities sent her mind into a whir. The note Jim had given to Charity the day before the tragedy, troubled her without end.

It read, 'Charity, you successful scholar! Now that you're going to Cambridge and we're parting ways, if I never see you again, know that you're very special to me.' She kept this a secret, as much as her love for Jim.

A light lunch was served, following the committal, where well-wishers had the opportunity to personally offer their words of sympathy. Some of these included neighbours of the two girls. Afterwards, on her way home with Charity, Lily kept hearing the minister's words. He had approached them and shook their hands offering his condolences.

Charity didn't seem touched by the minister's message at all. She was lost in sorrow and remorse and was unresponsive. Her puffy eyes were now hidden behind her black sun glasses.

Lily found refuge in her flat after the journey home. She needed some quiet time to reflect on her life and its direction. There had to be purpose to her being spared death, she thought. Was it just to go to law school, get a career, family and die later or in between? Or was there a missing ingredient, a missing link that made it more meaningful. Looking around the living room, her eyes rested on the coffee table.

Now for the first time in her life, Lily reached for the Bible, wondering if it would make any sense to her. As she opened it, her eyes rested on the words, "And He opened their understanding that they might comprehend the Scriptures."[10]

She was amazed that she could find an answer so soon by opening this book and was instantly convicted that she had denied the reality of God. Lily got down on her knees, there and then by the sofa, and cried out to God, "I believe You are there, help me to understand You and trust You Jesus."

Suddenly and gently she felt a weight of care lift from her, a sense of acceptance engulfed her. Lily was unsure what to do, so she decided to read the entire twenty-fourth chapter of Luke's gospel. As she read, she began to understand about the resurrection of Jesus Christ.

Somehow, she knew that this Christ was with her in the room and she was irresistibly drawn to His presence. Lily did not feel afraid, but safe and secure with Him. She prayed once more, this time asking Christ to come into her heart, change her life and be with her always, so that she would know Him every day.

There was a deep sense of comfort, peace and love that poured into her heart. Overwhelmed by such emotion, she started to sing:

For me You were willing to suffer,
For me You were willing to die,
For me You were willing to leave
Your holy throne on high;
You descended to this fallen world,
You saw my soul as a precious pearl,
You sacrificed Your very life,
To save my soul from hell;
Knowing this I won't resist,
The love that You have shown,
I surrender my life to You Jesus,
I'm no longer my own,
You paid for me with Your blood,
Forgiven me, cleansed me,
Filled my heart with Your love,
That I might spend the rest of my life,
Loving You.

The lyrics and tune came effortlessly as if flowing from a well deep within her. Lily closed her eyes and reflected for a moment on the words she had just sung and the change of emotion in her heart.

She had been transported from utter grief at the loss of her dear friend to this new sense of peace and joy with a far greater friend. Feeling sleepy after a draining day, Lily changed her clothes, climbed into bed and fell soundly asleep.

♡ ♡ ♡

It was six o'clock the next evening when Charity stepped into *The Fox & The Hound.* Lily was seated at a non-smoking table and had ordered dinner. Charity was still in her colours of mourning, with smoky-grey eye shadow and mulberry lipstick, while Lily was dressed in brighter array of lime green and khaki, wearing natural toned make-up. The wind howled ominously outside.

"Sorry, I'm a bit late Lily, traffic was chock-a-block."

Lily smiled. The waiter set down a pot of tea and two dishes, one of lasagne, chips and salad, the other of fish and chips with mushy peas.

"Uhmmm, just what I needed," said Charity relaxing.

"Looks really good," Lily observed.

"Come to think of it," said Charity eyeing her, "so do you. You've got more colour, sleep well?"

"Yes, surprisingly, very well Charity. How about you?"

"Not much, I've been very restless at night, I keep getting flashbacks and I wake up in fear." Charity's eyes were filled with tears.

"O Charity!" Lily responded with empathy, holding her friend's hands. "It will take time for you to come to terms with everything, but don't blame yourself. Jim wouldn't want that remember?"

Charity nodded. They had talked about this many times since the tragedy with friends, family and counsellors. It was painful to discuss and even more to let go of this guilt that dogged her for allowing the drinking to go that far. Still, Lily was right, Jim would disapprove of her self-recrimination. She remembered his favourite saying in their history classes, 'The past is past, let's learn from it and make a better today and tomorrow.'

"Are you taking anything to help you sleep?" Lily asked.

Charity shook her head and sighed. "I suppose I should try something; I didn't want to worry my parents. They think I'm about to fall apart, so I'm trying to show them that I can weather this storm."

"Well we both have suffered a major loss, but we'll get through it somehow. We can be strong together," Lily remarked with determination.

"You've certainly surprised me Lily, I was more concerned about you and here you are being the bigger shoulder for me to lean on. Something's definitely happened to you."

"I didn't realise it was that obvious."

"We've been friends for a long time now, Lily, I can sense when things are different, even when I'm feeling the blues."

"Well since I can't hide it, I might as well let the cat out of the bag. I took the step of faith I needed, to give my life more meaning Charity. I received Jesus as my Saviour last night."

"You *what?* You've not got religious overnight Lily, have you?"

"Well I don't know if you can call *me* religious, but I've... I've committed myself to Jesus and I believe that He's committed to me."

"Sounds like you need to be committed alright - to an institution!" Charity raised her right hand, shook her head and said, "No, I'm sorry Lily. I shouldn't have said that. It's not the time for sarcasm, but I just don't want to lose all my friends, okay and I don't care one iota about God, you know that and I would rather not talk about it."

"Charity you know I used to be the same. Off limits when God was mentioned, but you can see that I've changed. Don't you care about hearing why and what I experienced? Aren't we supposed to share heart to heart as friends?"

"Would you mind changing the subject to something we're both interested in?" Charity said with growing annoyance.

"Is that to say we shouldn't have talked about Sydney, since you were the one interested in him?"

"Sydney was a passing crush and that's different Lily."

"I don't think so. Anyway, how's your preparation for uni going?"

"Very well, I'm heading down next week to arrange accommodation and it's possible I might be getting a new car. Don't get me wrong I'm not wasting money, my old car is ready for a trade-in anyway."

"So how new is new?"

"One or two years old, my dad's helping me with it, sort of a leaving present."

"Jolly good! I'm reconsidering going to uni," Lily responded with some hesitation.

"What? Why would you do that? I was hoping we'd room together or at least study together." Charity looked at her friend with speculation.

"I think I need to take some time out and travel and possibly start uni next year."

"Lily, we agreed that we would not take a gap year. You had your heart set on going to university. I can't understand your change of mind. Does Jim's death have anything to do with it?"

"Partly... and something else."

"What?" Charity asked impatiently.

"I can't explain it, but I know that I need to pursue my relationship with Jesus Christ."

"You mean that your laying down your education because of *religion*?"

"*No*, I am taking a break because of Jesus. He is a person not a religion and He laid His life down for me, for you, for all of us and right now I think He's worth studying about more than anything else."

"Well why don't you come and take religious studies then?" Charity asked with agitation.

"Charity, it's not an academic endeavour; it's... it's a spiritual journey. No, it's not like going to Mecca or Jerusalem, but it's just winding down from the world of lectures, exams and clubs. I want a new life experience and I think I'm going to start attending church."

"*Church?*" Charity repeated incredulously. "Lily White, I never thought you'd come to this. I thought we were best friends. We used to do everything together. Are you going to spend more time with this Jesus than *me*?"

"Charity, I'm still your friend. My faith in Jesus shouldn't threaten you."

"Fine friend you are. We've just lost Jim. We shouldn't be going separate ways at a time like this!" Charity was beside herself, feeling angry and betrayed. She continued, "If you had to choose between friendship with me and this Jesus, who would you choose?"

Lily looked Charity in the eye, weighing up the situation, not liking the discord between them in the least. This was not what she had in mind for this evening. Why was Charity so aggressively against God? Lily actually saw her old attitudes reflected in her friend. It would take more than words to break down her resistance. She was just a day-old believer and her faith was already on trial.

Although Lily had experienced only one encounter with Jesus, she innately knew that Jesus was the most important person in her life. Charity was special and very close to her heart, but Jesus now possessed her heart.

With careful consideration and unnatural boldness she gently replied, "Charity I really wish you hadn't asked that question. You may not believe this - it's hard for even me to believe, but I just know that Jesus means more to me than anything else, He died for me!"

To this Charity blurted out, "You would choose some *historic* figure over a real life flesh and blood friend? Very well, consider me *history* as of tonight. Pun intended!"

Charity then got up defiantly and stormed out leaving her meal half-eaten. Lightning suddenly struck the pub and thunder boomed outside, leaving Lily quite shaken, bewildered and forsaken. She wanted to run after Charity, but she just sat dumbfounded. Unknown to Lily, the hound of heaven was in, with and behind her all that day.

Lily decided to walk home. She was drenched by the time she reached her flat. She had been crying in the rain. After a hot bath and some peppermint tea, she sought solace in her bed. Her eyes spotted the Bible, which she opened and found herself in the book of Luke again. This time, chapter nine. The twenty-third verse held her gaze. She began to read the passage before her.

Then He said to them all, "If anyone desires to come after Me, let him deny himself and take up his cross daily, and follow Me.

"For whoever desires to save his life will lose it, but whoever loses his life for My sake will save it.

"For what profit is it to a man if he gains the whole world, and is himself, destroyed or lost?

"For whoever is ashamed of Me and My words, of him the Son of Man will be ashamed when He comes in His own glory, and in His Father's, and of the holy angels.

"But I tell you truly, there are some standing here who shall not taste death till they see the kingdom of God."

Pausing at verse twenty-seven, she pondered these words and asked for understanding. Lily read some more, all of chapter ten and then turning the pages, she lighted upon the book of Matthew, chapter twenty-two. Lily was quite intrigued by what she read and longed to learn and discover more about God's kingdom.

She decided to pray and asked God to reveal the knowledge of His kingdom to her. Lily ended her prayer with thanks, having cast her friendship cares on Him, she then settled under the covers. In minutes she was fast asleep.

3

Rags to Righteousness

"By night on my bed I sought the one I love" [11]

What occurred next was quite momentous for Lily. This was an unusual dream, so vivid, so real. Lily found herself on a beach. Charity lay in rags on the shore beside a canoe. Jim's humped, sandy grave was right beside her. Lily shuddered at the sight. Charity had fallen asleep while sunbathing. As far as the eye could see, the people were dressed in rags, herself included.

There were rags of every colour and description, designer rags, common rags, custom-made rags, home-made rags. Footwear consisted of flip-flops, plimsolls and leather or nylon sandals. Before her was a wooden sign which identified the area as *The Kingdom of Rags*. Ahead of her lay, *The Kingdom of Righteousness*. She could see a beautiful mansion, a palace of some sort in the distance.

For some reason unknown to her, she believed that she belonged there. She promptly became aware of a man who was near her and strangely he was not dressed in rags. Lily couldn't discern what he looked like, she could see that he was wearing some kind of shimmering robe and sensed that she could trust him.

She wanted to ask him if she could go to the other kingdom, but dared not approach him in her rags. How could she ever go *there* like this? At the first opportunity, Lily purposed to get changed.

As if he read her thoughts, the man suddenly lifted her up in his arms and kissed her forehead. She seemed to melt in his embrace and he carried her to *The Kingdom of Righteousness*. He kissed her again as they crossed the threshold after ascending the marble stairs of the palace.

He took her up another flight of stairs and opened a solid, oak door and entered a large room where he gently placed Lily on a single bed covered with a new, soft, purple sheet. He gave her a goodbye kiss and left. Each kiss Lily received was pure, not sensual, disarming her of any resistance to the journey.

This person must be holy, Lily thought to herself. Overcome with delight that her desire to enter this land had been fulfilled, she quickly fell asleep. A powerful and majestic voice awakened her. She opened her eyes to see a brilliant light flood the room. It seemed as if the voice circled her as she listened.

"My Spirit brought you here Lily. He is the Holy Spirit, also known as the Holy Ghost, the Guide, the Comforter, the One who seals you as My own. He filled your heart with peace and love, when you asked Me to come in.

He loved and lifted you into My Father's house. I have promised you Lily that in My Father's house are many mansions. I have prepared a special room for you. So arise, come away with Me, My love."[12]

Even though Lily could not see Him, she realised that this was Jesus speaking and she responded, "How can I find or follow You, Jesus?"

"My Spirit is in your heart, listen to My voice and follow Me. I will lead you through many rooms. Come and follow Me."

Lily arose and didn't notice that she was still wearing her rags. She was led out of the room marked, *Reception,* to an adjoining room with a metal nameplate on the plain, unstained wooden door which was inscribed with the word, *Forgiveness.*

Inside this new room, she saw giant white movie screens on the earth-coloured walls. The floor was lined with red carpet. An unstained, wooden chair with a red cushion was in the middle of this room. Lily sat down and immediately on the left wall, the screen lit up with images from her past, of things she thought were best forgotten.

The Voice in her heart spoke and said, "Indeed your sins are forgotten, but only because I have forgiven you of them and their causes."

The middle screen lit up to show the crucifixion of Jesus, such scenes that she could scarcely behold them. What Lily saw moved her to tears.

"Lily," came the Voice again, "I had to die this way to provide forgiveness for you and all humanity. You are completely forgiven of your sins by My blood. Your heart is made new; I know that you love Me."

The screen flashed three verses - 1 John 1:9

If we confess our sins, He is faithful and just to forgive us our sins and to cleanse us from all unrighteousness.

Then appeared 1 John 2:1, 12

My little children, these things I write to you, so that you may not sin. And if anyone sins, we have an Advocate with the Father, Jesus Christ the righteous.

I write to you, little children because your sins are forgiven you for His name's sake.

Jesus then instructed Lily to believe and obey His voice. The right screen lit up with the images of people who had wronged her. Some she knew, some she didn't, some she couldn't remember. She was aware that she still had resentment towards them.

Next followed the verses:

Therefore as the elect of God, holy and beloved, put on tender mercies, kindness, humility, meekness, longsuffering;

Bearing with one another, if anyone has a complaint against another; even as Christ forgave you, so you must also do. Colossians 3:12,13

"Do you understand what this means Lily?"

"Yes Lord," Lily replied. "You want me to forgive those who have wronged me."

"And when necessary forgive yourself too," the Lord commanded.

The next room she entered had an iron door which was marked *Acceptance*. This room was furnished with citron yellow carpet, an iron chair with a matching yellow cushion and there were two huge screens on the grey walls. The first revealed scenes of Lily's past where she had struggled to believe in God.

Conversations with her parents and Mrs. Hopkins were shown. Jim's funeral service followed. It culminated with her cry to God for help and understanding. The acceptance that she had experienced before flooded her again and then the second screen came on. It showed times in her life when she felt rejected and unloved, forsaken and dismissed. These events were past and even future.

The voice of God reassured her, "You are accepted in the beloved Christ forevermore. I will never leave you Lily, neither will I forsake you."[13]

Just then the image of Charity's departure came up and then quickly disappeared. Jesus continued, "You have been faithful to Me; I will always be faithful to you, My love."

"Thank You for wanting me Lord and showing me that You care. Your perfect knowledge of me is so amazing. I'm finding comfort and security in Your omniscience."

With that, Lily arose and entered the room with the glass door marked, *Adoption.* Immediately lurking fears surfaced in her mind that she was not who she thought she was. In some sense this was true. Lily would yet discover her true identity.

There were four screens in this room with black carpet. After she sat down on the glass chair with jet black cushion, the room grew darker and she suddenly felt alone.

"I am with you," the Lord reminded her.

The first screen showed images from Creation. The darkness was suddenly pierced with the voice of the Lord as He spoke, "Let there be light."[14]

It seemed to Lily that the light was in the room with her, the very light that came into the earth, which shattered the darkness and had come into her heart!

Darkness fell, and then screen two lit up with the scene of her life in her mother's womb. It was very dark and then she saw herself moving down the birth canal and then, the first rays of light bursting upon her tiny form and her eyes. To her relief, it was her own beloved mother who had given birth to her.

Screen three came alive with another baby being born, the mother was in contractions. At birth, the baby was wrapped in swaddling cloths and put in a manger. Lily gasped at seeing the birth of Jesus before her eyes.

The scene changed to the garden of Gethsemane. There she saw Jesus in contractions, praying to His Father, sweating blood. The crucifixion appeared again. This time she experienced the period of daylight darkness. She felt alone and horrified at first, but then remembered her heavenly Father's words, "*You are accepted in the beloved Christ forevermore. I will never leave you Lily, neither will I forsake you.*"

The silence was broken with Jesus' declaration, "It is finished!"[15]

At that moment she saw the curtain in the temple torn in two from the top to the bottom. It reminded her of the baby coming through the birth canal. The last screen revealed more darkness, then the faint light of a spirit entering the atmosphere and finding itself in the womb of a woman. Next there appeared a bright Spirit infusing the spirit which had become dark. A hand then lifted up this spirit far above the heavens.

She somehow knew this was her spirit being raised up by the Spirit of God, just as he had lifted her up and brought her into *The Kingdom of Righteousness.*

Then God spoke, "Lily, I lovingly created you and purposely chose you, knowing that you would choose Me. Nothing about you or your concerns can be hidden from Me. I made you in My image to know and reflect Me. I love you and sent My Son into the world so that you could be a bona fide member of My family. You are My adopted child. My chosen vessel, My born-again daughter. I love you dearly. I, My Spirit and My Son live in your heart. You will never again be separated from Me - remember this!"

"Yes, Father," Lily replied in awe. The room grew exceedingly bright as He spoke, divine light embraced her being. She had never felt so loved and wanted as she did then. "Thank You Father, for adopting me."

Outside of this room, Lily discovered a narrow hallway with shimmering, turquoise walls that resembled gentle waves at the beach. There was no carpet, but a thick, glass floor with crystal clear water flowing beneath it.

At the end of the hallway stood a transparent lectern with a glass of water on its midway, built-in shelf and a huge open, brown, leather bound book on the top with gilded pages. Lily stood around the lectern and looked curiously at the open page and was very surprised to see her own reflection on the page.

She seemed rather plain without her make-up on, she thought to herself. Feeling thirsty she took a sip of water from the pastel pink vintage pressed glass stored beneath. The image on the page abruptly changed to reveal a scruffy, dishevelled girl, getting dirtier by the moment.

After that a glorious face appeared, so beautiful and bright, Lily had to shut her eyes. This all occurred in the space of seven seconds. The last image to appear was her reflection again. A light appeared at her feet, coming from the gold door behind the lectern. Awestruck, Lily turned the gold knob on this door and was ushered by the brilliant light into a room labelled, *Rejoicing*.

Upon entering this room, she could see a man clad in sunshine with rays of glory streaming from Him in every direction. He smiled at her, but she could not look at Him directly and so Lily closed her eyes. She then felt His hand touch hers and was gently whisked away into a waltz over the marble floor as He joyfully sang over her:

I have chosen you, I delight in you,
I want to be with you,
You are My resting place,
For Me to embrace,
Forever I'll dwell with you,
For I delight in you.

He spun her around and then continued:

I will abundantly bless your provision,
I will satisfy you with My bread,
I will clothe you with My salvation,
You will shout for joy as we wed.

I have chosen you, I delight in you,
I want to be with you,
You are My resting place,
For Me to embrace,
Forever I'll dwell with you,
For I delight in you.[16]

Lily found herself in a state of rapture as they danced. He looked at her tenderly and guided her to the exit so that she could step into the next phase of His plan.

4

The Garden of Freedom

"Draw me." [17]

Outside this room, Lily found herself in a beautiful garden. "This is the *Garden of Freedom,"* the Voice said in her heart. "You are now embarking on a journey of maturity Lily, through this Garden. You will be leaving the Palace grounds, but you will not be alone. To get to your destination you must follow *The Narrow Trail* only. Remember, I am with you always - follow Me."

As Lily gazed in wonder at the extravagant beauty of the Garden, everywhere she looked was a delightful explosion of colourful trees and flowers, picturesque topiary and manicured lawns. She began walking down *The Narrow Trail* where she came across a clear, sparkling river. It was signposted, *The River of Life.* Lily looked at her reflection in the river and saw herself dressed in a lovely, white, linen robe. Then she looked down at her own body and saw herself in the same common, yellow rags and pale green flip-flops she was wearing when she left *The Kingdom of Rags.*

Unable to reconcile the two images, she asked for understanding. The Holy Spirit spoke in her heart and revealed to Lily, that the river provided her true reflection - the robe she saw was actually on her, but it was invisible to her natural eyes because of the veil of her human flesh.

In reality, she was clothed in the beauty, holiness, righteousness and glory of God. It was a spiritual adornment, a supernatural draping. It was essential that Lily walk by faith, trusting God's word and not be led by appearances. To see her true self would require faith. Lily didn't know as yet how important this command would be to her maturity.

She had passed from rags to righteousness, from darkness to light, from trusting in her own ability and power to the ability and power of God. Lily sighed. She sensed this was not going to be an easy journey, but travelling with the Lord, she knew it would be safe. She was not to depend on her natural senses, but to walk in the realm of the spirit, to depend on the Holy Spirit to lead and teach her.

Further along she came across a large pond strewn with water lilies. To Lily's surprise, there was an ebony swan swimming in the pond. Lily never conceived there could be such a thing as a black swan, except one exposed to an oil slick. She was accustomed to seeing only white ones. As she stared at the unusual bird she was startled to hear it speak.

"Were you staring at my beauty, young lady?" The bird queried.

"You can talk?" Lily said taken aback.

"Of course I can talk! I'm not just a pretty beak."

Lily continued to stare at the bird in disbelief and found herself speechless.

"Out of interest, where did you get those threads?" enquired the swan.

"I'm not sure, I woke up in them," Lily replied sheepishly.

"Really! That is a pity isn't it?" continued the swan.

Lily was not so sure what to say, as she did think it a pity too, so she said nothing.

"Hel-lo? Anyone in those rags?" asked the bird rather mockingly.

"Rags! If only you knew the truth of the matter," Lily shouted in defence.

"I know that my name is Black Beauty," said the swan in a smooth voice.

"You mean like the horse?" engaged Lily curiously.

"I'm no horse indeed. There are different kinds of beauty in the world, Raggedy One."

"My name is Lily!" Lily exclaimed a bit irritated.

"My lips are naturally painted red," the swan continued self-absorbed, "it's plain to see that I am the most beautiful of all creatures; but you are covered in rags, such a shameful sight!" The swan was swimming in circles as it conversed. "Why don't you use some leaves for colour?" the bird suggested while pointing its slender neck in the direction of the fig tree.

Lily looked at the tree. Strangely it had leaves of every imaginable colour! She looked at her reflection in the pond and she appeared no different. Puzzled, she then decided to take a closer look at the tree completely mesmerised by the novelty of it all. Having picked a golden leaf, she wondered how she could use it.

Just then, a pure white dove landed on Lily's shoulder and said, "Remember the word of the Lord. He has clothed you in His regal robes, you are to walk by faith and not by sight." The dove then flew away.

The swan laughed, "I know what I can see, Lily, do not deceive yourself, the evidence is clear."

Lily understood and took heed to the dove's counsel as she dropped the leaf on the ground. She wanted to follow her Lord more than her desire to change her outward appearance. Before she had time to celebrate her victory over the swan, she was interrupted.

"Hey, watch what you're doing young lady!" a voice declared below Lily, pulling her away from her own thoughts. A forest-green caterpillar with a head at both of its ends greeted her downward gaze. "You weren't watching what you were doing, were you?" she was asked.

"No, I wasn't," Lily apologised. "I'm sorry I didn't see you."

"Not many folk do," said the other end of the caterpillar.

"Are you Siamese?" Lily asked.

"Sire who?" the end replied.

The other end shook its little green head and said, "I can't make head nor tail of what you're saying, but please watch your step!"

"Indeed," said the other end. "Don't you go dropping things either! It takes a lot of instinct to keep out of harm's way."

"Without a doubt. It's deeds like yours that decrease our numbers. It's no use having eyes at the back of one's head if they're covered up. But I'm not going to be down on the ground forever you know," said the caterpillar with great confidence. "I've got a bright future ahead of me."

The other end added, "Yes, I believe that one day I will be seated in heavenly places. I've been promised a good end and a hope of better things to come. Though I'm down, I'm not out. I'm going to be coming up one day. You'll see," finished the caterpillar, who then cheerily crawled away.

Lily stared with amusement at the double-headed, creeping creature as it moved along, then made her way further down *The Narrow Trail* and soon came to a fork in the road.

She read the sign above which stated, *The Good Samaritan Way.* Her attention was diverted by the sound of groans and a cry for help coming from the direction of the wide trail. The cry intensified and Lily felt she must see if she could be of help. Wasn't the Good Samaritan commended by Jesus, she thought, knowing that she had read of it in the Bible. After all she couldn't just think about herself, Lily reasoned. She followed her senses and left *The Narrow Trail* and headed in the direction of the cries.

As Lily rounded the bend, she could see a slim man lying in the road up ahead. He was moaning and groaning. She quickened her pace and found him in tatters with bruises and swelling. Bending over him, she felt a sharp blow to her head and immediately blacked out.

She awoke sometime later with a pounding headache, her rags partly torn, her body badly bruised. She felt cold and frightened. An unsettling fog had blanketed the area. Lily started to cry for help and heard movement towards her.

Two bald men, one thin and the other muscular, in black rags and sandals were approaching. They had an evil grin on their faces and were pointing at her while they laughed revealing both their mouths had some teeth missing. She soon realised that these were her attackers. Serpents and skulls were tattooed on their arms.

A sudden fear came upon Lily and she started trembling. What was she doing as a single woman on *this* road? One of the men, she identified as the man she had thought was injured. The bruises had been a make-up job. He had worn a black toupee which he was twirling in his hand. It had all been a cruel hoax!

They came much closer and said, "You got what you deserved. Only rebels travel the broad way." With a sly wink of their beady, dark eyes, they walked away laughing hideously in search of more game.

Weak and terribly hurt, Lily felt despair and deep shame closing in on her. A raucous cry pierced the air, as a crow circled above her. The crow taunted and condemned her of wilful disobedience and lust for self-rule.

The bird then pulled at her rags mockingly crying, "God resists the proud, your pride has brought you low. Lily you are ruined, you have no place to go." Round and round it flew with its condemning, damning chant.

Hope drained from her heart and in total desperation, Lily wept. She yearned for the Comforter and groaned for His help. Suddenly the dove reappeared and the crow fled from Lily.

"Lily, you called to Me. You are hurt and I am grieved. You must not forsake the path of righteousness. Stay on *The Narrow Trail* and you will not invite danger. I cannot lead you, if you choose to go your own way. You were vulnerable to the schemes of wicked men, who preyed upon your innocence and immaturity. I will deal with them at the proper time. You must not stray from the path I've given to you."

His words were bittersweet to Lily as she was passionate about justice and keeping laws.

"I am sorry," Lily said with deep remorse. "I thought I was doing good, but I was deceived."

"You must not depend on your senses, walk by faith dear Lily, not by sight."[18]

"Is there still hope for me? I feel so violated. Will it be possible for me to get back on *The Narrow Trail?*' she pleaded.

"Yes," replied the Comforter. "Understand this Lily, you are in Christ, and in Him there is no condemnation. I repeat, there is *no condemnation* in Christ. Do you admit your wrong?"[19]

"O yes, I know I went my own way and was disobedient."

"Then remember this, Christ is your Advocate, He has already paid for and forgiven you of your sins. His blood continues to cleanse you from all wrongdoing and your guilt. I will give you grace to return to *The Narrow Trail*. Once there, go straight to *The River of Life* and bathe."

Strength came to Lily's heart and she feebly stood up and hobbled back to *The Narrow Trail*. The fog had now cleared which made it easier to see the path. She made a beeline for the river and in its reflection, saw that her body was all spotted, but her white robe was clean. Words appeared on the water:

'Come now, and let us reason together, says the Lord, though your sins are like scarlet, they shall be as white as snow; though they are red like crimson, they shall be as wool. If you are willing and obedient, you shall eat the good of the land'[20]

As Lily entered the river, she felt embraced by God's love. In the river, she found healing for her wounds, cleansing for her body and the peace that comes from forgiveness. The water circled her washing away her guilt, shame, fear and pain.

She was fully restored and came out of the water full of joy and gratitude. She had experienced abundant life and not death or any haunting memories in this river.

"That was so reviving Lord, thank You for Your forgiveness and grace," Lily proclaimed. The dove reappeared and flew around her five times declaring, "Grace to you always, dear Lily." Her hair, body and clothes were now completely dry.

"Now walk worthy of your call Lily. The law of the Spirit of life in Christ Jesus *frees you* from the law of sin and death."[21a]

She looked again at her reflection in the river and to her delight, found that her body appeared spot-free.

"The cleansing blood of Jesus has been applied to your heart Lily. He provided the healing you have received because He too was wounded."[21b]

"Yes," Lily acknowledged. "I will stay in the light and not walk in darkness."

"Lily there's one more thing that you must do to stay out of darkness."

"What is it?" Lily queried.

"You must forgive your attackers."

"Those scoundrels! They're evil men! I can't; they abused me."

"You must forgive because you've been forgiven, walk in love not hate and you must love your human enemies as Christ loved you Lily when you were a sinner."

She was then reminded of the scripture –

Bearing with one another, if anyone has a complaint against another; even as Christ forgave you, so you must also do.

"It won't be easy, but I'll try," Lily consented, then she added, "Please help me to be genuine."

"Just be willing," replied the dove.

"Okay, I will. I forgive my attackers."

New strength came to Lily's heart and a genuine love for her enemies. The dove then instructed, "Now continue your journey, you are made whole."

A copy of the Bible was given to Lily by two black and blue macaws and she was exhorted to meditate on it as she walked.

As she opened the white, leather-bound Bible, her eyes rested on Matthew chapter seven, verses 13 and 14, which read:

Enter by the narrow gate; for wide is the gate and broad is the way that leads to destruction and there are many who go in by it. Because narrow is the gate and difficult is the way which leads to life, and there are few who find it.

"O dear," Lily mumbled, "I hope it's not *too* difficult a way. It will be easier to bear though than destruction."

Down *The Narrow Trail* she ran, ignoring *The Good Samaritan Way*. She hurried on till she came to another junction. The road that crossed over *The Narrow Trail* was marked, *Good Works Way*.

"None of that for me," Lily muttered, "I've learnt my lesson."

At that moment she could see a woman coming towards her from that way. "It can't be, but it is!" cried Lily.

Walking rather aimlessly, Charity Scarlett came in full view dressed in blue denim, designer rags and white plimsolls. She looked very pale and it was obvious she had been crying.

"Charity, whatever is the matter?" asked Lily.

"I never thought I'd see *you* again," Charity drawled and stopped, "doesn't matter anyway, my life is in a mess, my reputation could be tarnished forever."

"Why do you say that?" said Lily in grave concern, standing on *The Narrow Trail.*

"I didn't pay enough attention, it was an accident, but it was my own error and if she dies, I'll be guilty of manslaughter. I'll *never* be able to forgive myself." Charity put her right hand just below her nose, covering her mouth to hold back the tears. Her blonde hair was blowing in the gentle breeze.

"Who are you talking about?" demanded Lily.

"My patient, Lily, who else? I was working last night at the Infirmary and I administered the wrong dosage of medicine. Mrs. Johns' blood pressure shot up dramatically and she went into cardiac arrest. She's now in critical condition at St. Hugh's."

Charity burst out crying, holding her face in her hands. Lily wanted to comfort her, but purposely refused to trespass and leave *The Narrow Trail.*

"Please come closer," Lily requested.

"What difference does it make? I'm guilty of harming an invalid. I've got blood on my hands!" Charity wailed.

"Charity, though your sins are red like crimson, they can be as white as wool! You can be forgiven. God forgave me and I know He's no respecter of persons."[22]

The dove reappeared and perched on the street sign between them. A song could be heard in the wind:

Come, come to Me,
I want to set you free,
I can see that you are weary,
Your burden is so heavy,
Come, come to Me.

Come, come to Me,
I will give you rest,
So you can be refreshed,
In Me you will be blessed,
Come, come to Me.

Come, come to Me,
There's so much for you to learn,
My acceptance you can't earn,
You are loved, for you I yearn,
Come, come to Me.

Charity felt a flicker of hope as she listened. She straightened up, pushed her hair back and wiped her eyes and nose. Her heart began to soften and she responded, "Can I be forgiven Lily?"

"Yes, of course. Why don't you just come over here and I'll show you how." Charity moved towards Lily, having come to the end of herself, but just as she was about to pass over, a voice cried out her name frantically from behind.

"Charity, Charity Scarlett, Charity stop! I've got news," the breathless man shouted while pressing his bell.

Charity turned and saw a messenger on a bicycle and ran back down the broad trail to meet him. She took the letter he offered her and opened it. What she saw caused her to scream in anguish, "No! No!" then she fell into a heap on the path sobbing.

Looking on with deepening concern, Lily called to Charity to come back to her. In a sudden rage, Charity got up and yelled at Lily, "No! I will not come back. I have no hope of forgiveness from anybody now. I took this sick woman's life away."

"But..."

Before Lily could answer her, Charity concluded, "I'm going back to face the music, I cannot stop and talk now. My judgement awaits me." With utter despair in her heart she turned around and walked swiftly down the *Good Works Way*.

"She was this close to coming to repentance," Lily said in a whisper. "This close!"

The dove spoke comfortingly, "Many are called, Lily, but few actually make the choice." Then the dove departed.

Lily moved on, pained at the outcome of this surprise meeting. Still there was hope that Charity in her dilemma might call on God for help.

The air was fragrant with late blossoms from fruit trees and large, beautiful flowers that lined the narrow garden trail. The peonies, sunflowers, begonias and hydrangeas were in profusion. Lily could hear thrushes, larks, blackbirds, blue tits and robins singing from the trees and her spirit was lifted in the joy of their chorus.

She sat down on a stone wall and picked a golden apple from a tree nearby, her palate welcoming its juicy filling. Then looking around her with grateful pleasure, and up at the cloudless blue sky, Lily burst into inspired song:

Nothing I can see or smell,
Taste, touch or hear,
Can compare with the majesty of God.
Nothing I can see or smell,
Taste, touch or hear,
Can compare with the majesty of God.

When I look at the beauty of a bird or butterfly,
When I drink in the sights of a glorious sunset sky,
The green of the countryside or rushing waterfall,
I receive a witness as I hear creation call...

Nothing I can see or smell,
Taste, touch or hear,
Can compare with the majesty of God.
Nothing I can see or smell,
Taste, touch or hear,
Can compare with the majesty of God.

To smell the fragrance of a rose in full bloom,
To touch its petals filled with rich perfume,
To taste the food that I love to eat,
Is another reminder of the One who makes life sweet...

Nothing I can see or smell,
Taste, touch or hear,
Can compare with the majesty of God.
Nothing I can see or smell,
Taste, touch or hear,
Can compare with the *majesty* of God.

He is life's great purpose,
His name is Jesus,
The altogether lovely One,
The fairest of us all.

Nothing I can see or smell,
Taste, touch or hear,
Can compare with the *majesty* of God.

  With her head against the apple tree, Lily soon dozed off, resting in the shade from the heat of the sun.

5

Flashback

"Many waters cannot quench love" [23]

When Lily awoke, she could still hear the cheery singing of the birds. She got down from the wall and merrily continued her journey into maturity.

A large blue marquis piped in yellow was straight ahead. Lily looked at the venue with anticipation, eager to find out what she would encounter there. She stepped through the entrance to find an art exhibition displayed around the tent on canvas of different sizes. In the middle there was a semi-circular seating area which was nearly full.

The audience sat riveted to the artist Daniel DeVouz, dressed in a white shirt and blue dungarees, who was articulating how each piece was inspired. He was of slim build, tall and quite dashing to look at. Under his grey cap, his curly blonde locks framed an oval face with striking blue eyes. He beckoned her to a seat and continued his story about the portrait.

Lily noticed that every one sat attentive all dressed in different colour rags. A number of midgets were in the audience and appeared quite engrossed in the details being given. One however, seemed to sneer at her or was it just her imagination, she mused.

"That's all for now, let's stop for refreshments," Daniel declared.

Applause followed and waiters entered with trays displaying parkin, toffee apples, berry scones filled with butter or jam & fresh cream and bottles of still rhubarb & dandelion. It was a good thing that the refreshments were complimentary and Lily heartily took her fill. A waiter approached juggling his pears. She applauded him as he neared her chair.

"That was quite skilful!"

"Thank you and pleased to meet you, Poddles the name," he replied and offered his tray of pears.

Lily picked one and he handed her a paper bill which was actually a twenty pound note.

"You're paying me? That's quite a sum!"

"Consider it a gift," he winked and continued his juggling.

She looked again at the note, put it in her pocket and instantly found herself on a residential street at night in the rain. A number of lanterns lit the area and a young woman of similar age tapped her shoulder and offered her a red brolly.

"Not prepared are you?" the woman remarked looking at her flip-flops.

"Not in the least, it was all so sudden."

"I'm Beth, short for Elizabeth and you are?"

"Lily."

"Let's get you into shelter Lily," Beth suggested as she held Lily's hand.

Beth wore a yellow hooded mackintosh and purple paisley-patterned wellies. They ran together through the streets as the rain intensified and eventually climbed some steps and entered a terraced house.

"You can place the brolly by this coat rack," Beth said as she took off her wellies, then her raincoat and hung it on the rack. "Time for some tea and biscuits, that'll get us warm. Bring your flip-flops." Then she veered off to the left and opened the door to a cozy snug with a lit fire.

A pot of tea, cups and a plate of Scottish shortbread biscuits were laid out on a large tray on top of a brown pouffe. Beth smoothed her green cotton dress that had gotten a bit wrinkled. She was of medium brown complexion and her curly brown hair was in a ponytail; her dark blue eyes were focused on Lily. She sat on a tartan armchair and Lily still in her rags, sat on the one across from her. Lily offered to share her pear which was quite sweet and juicy in taste. There was a hint of lemon in the biscuits which Lily found quite delicious.

An ear-shattering scream filled the house and the two young women stared at each other then took off in the direction of the sound. In the kitchen they found a woman in hysterics wringing her hands. It was Beth's mother Mrs. Atkins. A crumpled letter lay on the tiled floor.

"Mother, whatever is the matter?"

A soft moan escaped her mother's lips as she nearly fainted, but Lily caught her. Beth picked up the letter her mother was staring at and read the message:

My dearest Sofia,

It pains me to confess that I have squandered our savings and have just been declared bankrupt. I had taken to drink while on the road and found it quite hard to give up my habit. I invested in a corrupt financial scheme when my head was not clear and have thoroughly been taken to the cleaners. I will not return as I don't even have the fare to do so and will not be able to abide your questions and disappointment in me.

I do hope in time you and Beth will be able to forgive me. I covet your prayers.

Earnestly yours
Duncan

Tears filled Beth's eyes and she looked up in despair to her mother.

"Whatever shall we do? Father needs to come home, at least the house is paid for, isn't it?"

Her mother nodded sadly as she released a deep sigh and shudder.

"Will you forgive him Mother?"

Mrs. Atkins swooned and Lily held her firmly and led her into the snug to sit down. Her straight dark brown hair was swept off her face in a neat wrap. Her eyes were a lighter blue than Beth's. Beth kneeled before her mother, who stirred and offered her some tea.

"Mother you gave me a fright, please have some tea and rest. We can talk about this later, ok."

Mrs. Atkins nodded again and was quite pale in appearance. Lily beckoned to Beth to leave the room.

"I'm sorry to be caught up in your private concerns, Beth. Would you like me to leave?"

"O no, your coming was quite providential. We'd both be worse off without you."

Lily silently asked the Comforter to visit this family and then spoke up. "Would you mind if I prayed?"

"Of course not, we need all the help God can give us."

Holding hands the two girls closed their eyes and Lily requested guidance, wisdom, provision and comfort for the Atkins' family. An idea suddenly hit her and she pulled the note out of her pocket.

"Please take this Beth, it may not go far, but it's a start."

"Are you sure?" she asked with surprise

"Definitely, you rescued me from the rain, the least I can do is offer you something in return. May God multiply it and restore your family."

Beth hugged her gratefully and said, "You are truly a godsend."

Lily smiled and replied, "We both are."

Lightning flashed at the kitchen window and in an instant Lily was in her seat again in the marquis.

A waiter approached with what seemed to be large white cubes on a tray with words all mixed up.

"Please choose one and see if you can unscramble it," he offered with a twinkle in his blue eyes

Lily looked at him and then the artist.

"I'm his brother Ron," the waiter said

"I can see your striking resemblance," she responded with a smile and then chose a cube.

He handed her a paper bill just like Poddles had. This note was worth fifty pounds.

"Goodness, that is a lot,"she responded

"And worth every penny," Ron said as he moved along.

She held it in her hands this time and in a flash she was back in the kitchen with Beth. A man's voice could be heard in the snug.

"Who's in there?" she asked.

"Officer Jones. My father was found collapsed with hypothermia. He's in St. Hugh's battling pneumonia," Beth said quite tearful.

"St Hugh's in Lincoln?" Lily asked while giving Beth a comforting hug.

"Yes, you know of it?" Beth queried.

"I was born there. Are you going to see him?"

"I hope so, money is scarce at the moment as you know. It will cost much to travel and we don't know if we'll have to stay in a B&B."

"I've got some more money," Lily said and produced the bill she received from Ron. "Take it and you can stay at my flat at Manor Views," she graciously offered.

Lily then realised she did not have the key and said, "You can ask my landlady Mrs. Spencer for a spare key, tell her I sent you. She lives in flat 3."

"O you are a dear, are you sure you want to do this?" Beth asked, incredulity evident in her voice.

"Nonsense, of course! What are friends for?" she smiled and squeezed Beth's hand.

"Please, come with us, you know the area," Beth pleaded.

"Oh all right, I do want to know how this turns out," she remarked.

At that moment Officer Jones approached to bid Beth goodbye, he nodded at Lily and was shown to the door by Mrs. Atkins.

"There you are, have you heard?" she asked Lily.

Lily nodded and offered to pray for the family. Mrs. Atkins agreed and they bowed their heads and she asked their heavenly Father to touch Mr. Atkins and heal him, strengthen and comfort the family, continue to guide and provide for them.

"Amen!" they said in unison and Mrs. Atkins heard of her gift and offer, then embraced her with gratitude.

♡ ♡ ♡

"He's stable, that's good," commented Mr. Silver. "Keep him on the drip. I will check on him tomorrow."

The consultant left the room and walked to the nurses' station. Charity looked at Mr. Atkins with much disdain, never one to have compassion on the less fortunate even though she had chosen this profession. Treat the down and out she would, but not sympathise with their sorry circumstances. After all, he had caused this misfortune, if what he had mumbled in his delirium was true. She closed the curtains, picked up her clipboard, made some notes and moved on to attend to Mrs. Johns.

♡ ♡ ♡

Mrs. Atkins stood on the platform at Waterloo station watching the clock. Two suitcases were between her and Beth. One with clothing and effects for Mr. Atkins, as well as her things. The other had Beth's selected belongings. The train approached a crowded station and they huddled together and boarded in the middle. The open economy tickets were not too expensive and they sat together. Beth sat beside her mother and Lily sat with a kind stranger, an elderly gentleman with bushy eyebrows and curled moustache who offered to pay for their refreshments after enquiring the reason for their trip.

"Ghastly thing, pneumonia, but if his constitution is strong, he will recover," Mr. Parkinson stated.

Mrs. Atkins nodded with a weak smile.

"Mind you, my father was in the war and suffered that and worse and made it back, so keep your hopes up," he added kindly, then asked, "may I offer you something more in terms of assistance?"

The three looked at him, their curiosity piqued.

"Here you are, this should do," he said as he opened his wallet and took out a wad of notes and handed it to Mrs. Atkins.

Colour drained from her face and then immediately returned as he laughed and shook his head. Beth and Lily were just as stunned at his generosity and looked from Mrs. Atkins to Mr. Parkinson.

"One must share and share alike," he remarked pressing the notes into her hand and added, "I couldn't think of a better family I would like to be a benefactor to, our meeting was quite providential wouldn't you say?"

"Yes, quite," piped up Beth.

"Indeed it is," answered Mrs. Atkins, recovering from her initial shock and having found her voice.

"Thank you Mr. Parkinson, journeying beside you has been an unexpected pleasure," remarked Lily.

"Well ladies," he said gathering his things which consisted of a walking stick, tan leather briefcase and a dark grey coat, "The pleasure is all mine and godspeed to you all, this is my stop."

With handshakes and a wave he stepped off the train and disappeared into the waiting crowd.

"Just three more stops, Mother," Beth stated.

"Beth, I think we're going to be all right. God has answered our prayers so far," she said with a smile.

♡ ♡ ♡

"How is he doing today?" Mr. Silver asked Charity as she was preparing to leave having finished her shift.

"Slept most of the night, only had one faint outburst, muttering to himself then fell asleep again," she replied. "His drip has been replenished and his vitals are still stable."

"Good we're making progress. Goodbye Miss Scarlett,"

"Goodbye Mr. Silver," Charity said putting on her coat and then she walked purse in hand to the lift. As the doors pinged open to her surprise she saw Lily step out with the other occupants. She tried to avoid further contact, but in vain.

"Charity, long time no see," said Lily quite happily.

"I'm on my way home, it's been a long night and time for me to get some sleep." She responded abruptly.

"You were visiting someone?" Lily asked kindly.

"No! I'm working here, some drunk with pneumonia was brought in and I've been seeing to him and others. Now I have to be on my way, as I said, it's been a long night."

With that Charity entered the other lift and the doors promptly closed as Lily bade goodbye to Charity.

"Friend of yours Lily?" Beth asked.

"We used to be best friends actually. I wonder if she was attending your father?"

"Let's find out," Mrs. Atkins suggested and headed towards the nurses station.

"If she wasn't' in a rush we could have found out from her," Lily reflected.

"Her description was far from kind in my opinion," Beth remarked.

They followed Mrs. Atkins with the suitcases and were led by a nurse to a room at the far end of the hall. Mr. Atkins was awake. He appeared to be very thin and weak. His greying hair was close cut and his dark grey eyes looked tired. Mr. Silver greeted them and advised it was ok to stay for a while but not ask many questions of the patient. He took Mrs. Atkins aside and spoke with her privately.

"Father," greeted Beth as she rushed to his bedside and sat on a chair. "I've missed you. How are you feeling?"

"Better than before, all for seeing you," he weakly replied then coughed.

"This is Lily, a new friend, she's been praying for you," Beth said as she introduced her.

"Very kind of you lass to do so. Thank you," Mr. Atkins said with ragged breath.

"Pleased to meet you Mr. Atkins," Lily replied.

Mrs. Atkins looked with concern at her husband as the consultant continued speaking with her and then left.

"Duncan dear," Mrs. Atkins said as she approached him, "you had me so worried, I was beside myself when I read your letter and then heard you had been admitted. How are you?" She reached for his hand.

"Glad and sad to see you, only because I put you through all this...," he uttered.

"Hush now, we will talk and get through this, concentrate on getting better for now. Okay?"

He nodded as tears filled his eyes and his wife kissed his cheek. She pulled tissue from a box on the side cabinet and dried his eyes.
Beth motioned to Lily that they should leave the room.

"Be back in a bit," she said to her parents and closed the door.

"Am I in the way?" Lily asked self-consciously.

"Not at all Lily, they just need some space from both of us."

They sat in the waiting area at the other end of the corridor. Lily took off the green parka Beth had loaned her and retrieved the cube she had placed inside.

"I'm glad you're both reunited with your father."

"Me too. I'm glad for your company as well Lily."

Lily looked at her and smiled, twisting the cube.

"Can I have a go at that?" Beth offered.

"Sure, the more help the better."

"Uhmm let's see," said Beth as she lined up some letters. "I'm fascinated with words and have a keen eye, I've been told by friends."

"Found anything yet?" teased Lily

"Sure, the words 'stoop' and 'soar'," Beth said triumphantly.

"Good advice. Seems you're off to a flying start," Lily chuckled.

"I like the pun," smiled Beth. "Now it's your turn."

Lily took the cube and tackled another side with twists and turns.

"I've found 'acts' and 'kindness'!" Lily said with glee.

"Hurrah!" said Beth as she was handed the cube.

After a few puzzling minutes two more words were discovered.

"I've got 'wisdom' and 'love'."

"Good, you'll need them, trust me," Lily remarked and they both laughed.

On her final attempt, she clapped her hands with delight and said, "Best portion."

"A fitting finale," cheered Beth with a bow.

Lily chuckled and they stood up and returned to the room. As they reached the door Mrs. Atkins opened it to reveal her husband had fallen asleep. Beth entered and kissed her father's forehead.

"Sleep well, Father, see you tomorrow," she whispered.

"'Bye Mr. Atkins," Lily whispered.

As they walked to the lift Lily remembered Charity and wondered if she had been absolved since she was still employed here. It also occurred to her that she herself could have been transported in time to possibly prevent the crisis. Either way, Lily hoped to cross her path again with more time to converse and find out how Charity was and if she had a change of heart.

It had started to rain as they neared the hospital entrance and Lily was glad Beth had insisted she bring the brolly. Mrs. Atkins had called for a taxi to take them to a nearby hotel which worked out well with the funds they received from Mr. Parkinson. They piled into the navy Nissan as the rain pelted the vehicle and sidewalk.

"Where to?" the driver enquired.

"Rendezvous Inn," Mrs. Atkins replied.

Lightning flashed and again Lily was transported to the marquis instantaneously. She was seated in the same chair with the cube in hand minus the fifty pound note, parka and umbrella. Curiously she inspected the cube and found that the discovered words were still intact.

"Amazing," she declared.

"I couldn't agree more," a voice behind her said.

Lily turned her head to see Ron standing with an empty tray and a wide grin.

"Thank you for joining us today, the exhibition has now finished and as you can see," he said as he gestured with his hands pointing to the departing audience, "It is time to go."

Lily promptly got up, picked up her Bible and Ron examined her cube and said, "It's been worth the trouble hasn't it?"

"Au contraire, no trouble at all. I found it all very exciting and adventurous. Keep it."

"I trust you have benefited from our encounter then."

"More than words can say," Lily replied with a twinkle in her eye.

Daniel DeVouz approached and extended his hand. Lily took it and after they shook hands, he straightened his cap and clapped his hands.

"Thank you all once again for your attendance and attention. I have enjoyed having you here and hope to see you again in the near future."

Lily took a quick look at the beautiful scenic and portrait paintings before she exited the tent. Outside the crowd had dispersed and she found herself alone again as she continued on the trail.

6

Iona

"Like a lily among thorns" [24]

"Message for Lily White, message for Lily White," announced the messenger's call behind her.

Lily turned around to see the same messenger of doom that had appeared earlier, coming her way with a letter in his hand. She felt anger towards this young man and knew that she would have to deal with her emotions. Lily stopped and he handed the letter to her.

Curiously she opened it, recognising the handwriting as Charity's. She recalled her encounter at St. Hugh's. The messenger waited, adjusting his navy blue cap which matched his ragged shirt and shorts. Pinned on his shirt was a white, triangular badge bearing the letters 'STC' also in navy blue, the letters stood for swift, timely couriers. The delivered letter read:

Dear Lily
For want of a better salutation! I have had some time to think over my predicament for which I am very glad. In my state of emotional weakness, I nearly fell into your religious trap, but I was saved by the messenger's bell. To think that you would try to take advantage of me, makes me no more guilty than you. I don't ever want to see you again Lily.

As for your God, who needs his forgiveness? I have been very charitable, volunteered my services and helped others the best I could. My great regrets are Jim's death and my recent blunder, but put on the scales with my other good deeds - I'm sure to have it tip in my favour.

I pity you Lily. You've become so narrow-minded, wasting your life on religious rubbish. What good is Jesus, if all he does is thwart your plans and dreams and separate friends. With a friend like him, who needs enemies?
Your ex-friend
Charity
P.S. You are a fool to follow Jesus. Mark my words. You'll end up with nothing. NOTHING!

Lily blinked away her tears as she finished reading. How cold, cutting and critical of Charity. "But did I do something to upset her?" Lily wondered aloud.

"Any reply?" the messenger interrupted.

"Not at the moment," Lily answered a bit indignant taking the pen and paper he offered.

"Very well," the messenger said and then left as hastily as he appeared.

Feeling wounded in spirit, Lily sat down. Reminiscing on the relationship she had with Charity, stirred in her a well of mixed emotions. She felt angry and sad at the same time.

"Why do things get so sour?" she pondered. "Our friendship has turned from wine into vinegar."

She opened the Bible for insight and direction. Matthew chapter five stared at her. While reading, she received comfort and guidance and she determined to be mature in her response.

"I will love my enemies, I bless those who curse me, I will do good to those who hate me and pray for those who despitefully use me and persecute me." [v44]

Lily was convicted that she didn't love the messenger and so humbly confessed her sin and prayed for him.

"Father, I pray that this STC employee will come to know You and be a bearer of good news. I shouldn't be prejudiced towards him because he was only doing his job."

In this frame of mind, Lily prepared to reply to Charity's letter:

Dear Charity,

I was pleased to get word from you after your hasty departure. However, I am not pleased with the way things have transpired between us. You have and always will be a very dear person to me and I will continue to consider you as my friend.

I must say that in no wise, did I seek to trap you and I'm very sorry you took it that way. I understand that we hold different points of view. In spite of your derogatory comments about Jesus and my commitment to Him, I choose to forgive you and affirm my resolve to love and follow Him. To be honest, I'd rather have Jesus and nothing else than to gain this world's goods and be without Him. 'For me to live is Christ.'[25]

Should you change your mind and wish to see me, I will gladly welcome your visit. I earnestly pray for your welfare and that you will put your life in God's hands. For everyone will give an account to God. Charity - all our good deeds are like filthy rags. To be right with God, it is imperative that you trust in Jesus and not your own good works.

Sincerely yours
With love,
Lily

It was a very long while before Lily had news of Charity again. By this time Lily had made good progress on her journey into maturity and steadfastly kept to *The Narrow Trail*.

She had tasted a variety of fruit - apples, pears, plums, berries, bananas and mangoes and enjoyed drinking the refreshing water from the springs. The weather was delightfully tropical and the views all around her were breathtaking.

Lily gave herself to prayer and busied herself reading all the Psalms and Proverbs, praising God as she travelled along, learning to walk in wisdom. In the distance was another intersection. They always seemed to be places of testing.

She recalled *The Narrower Trail*, she recently came across. There she had been tempted to take this seemingly spiritual path. The sign had a small print message which read, in brackets, 'quickest route for all journeys'.

On top of the sign was a peculiar and fascinating sight. A very tall, narrow, purple ladybird with pink spots and pink spectacles was holding a pink, thin toadstool umbrella with purple spots.

Having caught Lily's attention the creature declared, "Now that you've spotted me, have you decided to go express or the long way?" Then without allowing Lily to answer, the ladybird smiled and continued, "Rhetorical question really, here's your Journey Express traveller's card."

She then handed Lily a pink travel card and flew away. The card had purple spots and was quite pretty. Lily decided to take the route and just a short distance down this very narrow track she felt a sharp pain on her wrist. Looking down she noticed a diagonal cut twelve millimetres long.

"Ouch," she cried as the sting of the cut increased and blood seeped through the incision. It was then she paused for thought and decided to go back to the sign. A lamb was standing there wearing a navy blazer with brass buttons and a brown, wooden bucket around its neck. The ladybird was nowhere in sight.

"Hi there, I am Marcus, the Route Inspector, where are you headed Miss?"

"I'm on a journey to maturity," Lily replied while pressing her wrist.

"Well you can't get there by Express. There are no shortcuts to Maturity. No indeed. Only *The Narrow Trail* can get you there."

"So I've been told," she said in reflection.

"Well, hop to it, drop the card in this bucket and press your wrist against one of my hooves."

As Lily bent down, she noticed the bucket had more cards and that Marcus had many slash marks on his hooves. But before she could ask the question, he stated, "That's how many wayward travellers I have helped and healed, I bear the marks of their errs. Get on with it then miss!"

Spurred to action, Lily pressed her wrist against the lamb's back, left hoof and rose up to find her cut had stopped bleeding and was diminishing by the second. It vanished right before her eyes.

"Wow!" was her delighted remark, but then she was aware that Marcus too had disappeared. "Well I never! I do meet the most interesting creatures."

Lily breathed a prayer of thanks and was strongly cautioned by the Holy Spirit not to be led astray by counterfeit paths. The next distinct path was signposted *The Self-planned Way*. Walking past the sign, she noticed a newspaper spread on the broad trail. She could just about read the headlines:

'Medical student commits suicide after guilty verdict.'

Charity's picture was on the cover. Lily felt a sickening feeling rise in her stomach. She hurried on not wanting to be waylaid by her emotions.

Further down the road, she sat down by a well. Lily was shrouded with a sense of failure, grief and guilt. Weeping, she cried out to God for refuge. Lily had cared deeply for Charity and truly wanted her to be blessed. Now another friend's life was lost in tragic circumstances.

"My way is laden with sorrow and grief," she tearfully declared.

"As was Mine," came the voice of her Lord. "You walk a narrow path My dear, at times friendless, despised, mistreated by the world and loved ones. But remember I experienced this and more and have overcome. I will remain your closest friend and will never desert you. Follow Me now Lily to Iona. I have something important to reveal."

Lily stood up and followed the sign on *The Narrow Trail* which pointed to Iona. Once there she came across a mound holding three trees and three crosses, surrounded by a body of water.

The three trees were to her left in Iona. All were particularly beautiful. The first tree was labelled, *The Tree of Life,* the second, *The Tree of the Knowledge of Good and Evil* and the third, *The Tree of Sacrifice.* This last tree had two branches missing, which formed an altar in front of it. The horizontal branch rested on top of the vertical one. On the altar was an animal's skin.

"Choices were made at these trees Lily," the Lord advised. "Eve chose the fruit of the second tree and so did Adam. That is the source of all grief, pain, loss, sorrow and shame in the world. I chose the third tree as a prophetic remedy and temporary aid to the human tragedy. An innocent creature had to die to bring relief to man's soul, cover for the shame and means of forgiveness."

The Lord continued, "My desire was that they would have eaten from the first tree and not the second. Then there would be no need for the third. However, knowing beforehand their choice, I prepared the third tree for their salvation. See the three crosses?"

"Yes Lord," Lily answered.

"Point out to Me the parallel with the third tree."

After some thought Lily spoke up. "The middle cross where You were sacrificed."

"You have answered correctly. There were two thieves who hung beside Me. The cross to your left held the repentant thief; the right cross held the rebellious thief. Do you see the parallel with the other trees Lily?" the Lord questioned her again.

She considered the crosses and the trees. "I think *The Tree of the Knowledge of Good and Evil* relates to the cross holding the rebellious thief and *The Tree of Life* relates to the cross holding the repentant thief."

"You are right Lily. *The Tree of Life* is in Paradise and that's exactly where the repentant sinner goes. Read it now in Revelation chapter two, verse seven and Luke twenty-three, verse forty-three."

Lily opened her Bible and read the verses, then asserted, "It's just as You said!"

The Lord continued speaking to her as she looked at the crosses.

"Lily, when Adam and his wife sinned, I lost two close friends. Their sin separated them from Me.[26] Our *intimacy* was lost, breached, broken. I know what you are feeling."

Lily focused on the Lord as He continued, "In My hour of deep grief, I forever lost the friendship I desired with the rebellious thief, but on the other cross, eternally won a friend when that thief repented. Lily, the most important thing in life is *fellowship with Me*. Time spent with Me prepares you for everything else. It matters to Me that you finish the course I have set for you."

He stopped talking for a moment, then in a tender tone called to Lily.

"Yes, Lord?" she replied.

"You heard My voice and chose to follow Me. I'm very glad I didn't lose you. Stay close to Me Lily."

Moved with heartfelt emotion, a mixture of love and gratitude, Lily fell to her knees and wept. She had cried herself to sleep and upon opening her eyes, found no sight of the trees or crosses. Lily rubbed her eyes and looked again. They had somehow disappeared.

It dawned on her now that the middle cross was in her heart. She was truly willing to lay her life down, to die to her own wishes, take up her cross and lose everything for Jesus' sake - friends, fame and fortune, so that she could follow and know Him.

Lily got up, stretched and shook her rags. After straightening her flip-flops, she turned around and resumed her journey on the narrow path. A willing woman walking wherever the trail would lead.

♡ ♡ ♡

Lily walked some distance until she came to the next intersection. Though she rarely met any other traveller, she could clearly see that the track was well worn and used by those who went before her. The sign perpendicular to *The Narrow Trail* read, *Beat It.*

"How strange!" Lily commented, then she looked up in horror to see a tornado approaching, accompanied by a buzzing, roaring sound. Lily stood paralysed for a moment at the awful sight. She soon realised that this moving monster was an army of killer bees!

In mortal fear, she watched the swarm and resolved to get out of harm's way. However, her legs felt like jelly and she irrationally but wisely reasoned that she could not beat it, because it was proven folly to leave the path God had chosen for her.

Terror gripped her mind as she thought about the expected attack. She couldn't defend herself against the pending onslaught. The Bible she had would not suffice as a swat for a swarm or would it?

As the bees swarmed around her, Lily was caught up in the rhythm of their movement. Instead of stinging they were singing, friendly not fierce. She could hear them singing a proverb that drained away her fear and relieved her tense, tired muscles.

This was their song:

Will you be, can you be
True to your God?

To walk by faith
Whatever the cost
The narrow way is trod;
Tread the narrow way
Be true to your God.

They surrounded her as a wall of controlled fire, drawing her into their tuneful dance. Lily moved her head and feet to and fro as she danced with the bees. Then without warning, they flew above her head and changed their disposition. They moved like a pack of hungry and angry wolves. In cyclone formation they flew down the *Beat It* trail to execute judgement on those taking that route.

Lily shuddered when she realised how close she had come to death's door. "That was a narrow escape!" she said aloud and chuckled to herself about the pun. This journey was filled with the unexpected. She was thankful for the grace she had experienced in choosing to walk by faith.

God surely was looking after her, even when she didn't know what to do she could trust in His guidance. It was clear to Lily that she could not believe everything she saw or heard, she must be discerning and listen to God's voice. She looked at the Bible and then sighed again. This certainly was no easy stroll.

7

Passage Among Plants
"plants of the valley"[27]

Walking slowly Lily eventually found herself nearing a semi-circular grove. She sat down under an olive tree and rested from the heat. Myrrh bushes and short trees only seven feet tall - mainly fig, acacia and olive surrounded her. They formed an interesting arrangement and provided a measure of shade for travellers.

Closing her eyes, Lily reflected on her journey, pondering the course she was called to take. She later awoke to find her skin dripping with oil. It appeared that she had been anointed while she rested. Her heart was filled with joy and Lily spontaneously burst out laughing. She rubbed the oil into her skin and delighted in the fragrance.

While looking up at the tranquil cornflower-blue sky and at the surrounding trees, she noticed some ripe figs and was ready for a snack as her appetite had also awakened. Whenever she slept, Lily was not sure how much time had elapsed - be it minutes, hours or days for when she awoke it was always bright. Regardless of the length of time that had just passed, she felt refreshed with new strength for the journey.

A lovely aroma drifted her way and beckoned to her senses to find its source. Curious and energised, Lily left the grove and saw before her a breathtaking view. A spectacular field of flowers three feet high like a variegated, scented, high carpet was on *The Narrow Trail*.

There were tall, elegant lupins, orchids, irises, dahlias, antirrhinum and delphinium; pink and white lilies of the valley, fuchsias, lilies, amaryllis, sunflowers and more, such a host that left Lily in a state of delighted awe.

She buried her face in some freesias and went from flower to flower, sniffing and drinking in the beauty all around her. Her skin began to soak in the fascinating fragrance as she wandered in the floral field. Lily was about to occupy herself in some tulips when the flowers strangely started to ascend.

Slightly startled, Lily found herself looking at an extraordinarily attractive, hazel-eyed, blonde woman who was wearing the tulips as a hat. In fact her entire clothing was made of flowers!

From her head to her feet, she was arrayed in every kind of flower growing in the field. Only her face, palms and soles were not covered. Adding to Lily's amazement was the fact that the flowers were all fresh and seemed to be living on this peculiar woman. She smelled heavenly and smiled as Lily looked at her in wide-eyed wonder.

"Hello Lily, I'm the Perfumer. I'm very pleased that you have made it this far."

"How do you know my name?" Lily asked stunned.

"You'd be surprised at what I know," she answered somewhat mysteriously, then added, "I am the King's attendant. He informed me that you were on the way."

"The King?" Lily queried.

"Yes, He sent you on this journey, remember?" the Perfumer sweetly replied.

Lily nodded as she reflected on the King and how He had greatly blessed her life bringing her into His kingdom. The Perfumer then invited her to sit in the field and share some floral juice. Lily drank the colourless liquid she had been given in a sturdy giant buttercup and quite enjoyed the taste. Then she was encouraged to tell the Perfumer about her travels.

At times, she was saved from going into detail as her listener would fill in the gaps, revealing her intimate knowledge of Lily's journey. It was a pleasure to have someone again in physical flesh to talk to about her experiences. Even though the Comforter was always with Lily, she neglected His companionship when she was caught up with cares and her own thoughts.

Whenever Lily praised God and expressed gratitude to Him, she released a sweet incense that perfumed the atmosphere. This had always been the case, but Lily had never been aware of this reality before. In the presence of the Perfumer, such spiritual things had a natural expression.

As Lily shared her adventures, her countenance shone and she was being changed from one degree of glory to another. Her testimony about God's activity in her life had in itself great power. Night fell for the first time on her journey and the two women drifted to sleep in the fragrant field.

Lily was awakened by a gentle, humming sound. She opened her eyes to find herself in a literal flower bed. Her head was resting on a soft butterscotch-yellow pillow, the centre of this flower. The magenta, velvet sheets covering her body were the petals of an enormous peony. As Lily moved, the petals opened of their own accord. To say that she was fascinated was no small truth.

To her left, among the hibiscus and other tropical flowers, a flock of iridescent hummingbirds were having breakfast. The rhythmic cadence of their wing-beat inspired Lily to sing a new song to the Lord as follows:

At dawn I arise; I look in Your eyes,
My mouth's filled with praise as I realise
You've been waiting for me, so patiently
Now You beckon me to come away with You.

Face to face, mouth to mouth
Heart to heart, life to life
You bring me closer
Face to face, mouth to mouth
Heart to heart, life to life
You bring me closer to You.

In every moment of every day
I sense Your presence and so I pray
You're talking with me, so intimately
I gladly choose to come away with You.

Face to face, mouth to mouth
Heart to heart, life to life
You bring me closer
Face to face, mouth to mouth
Heart to heart, life to life
You bring me closer to You.

From the other end of the field, the Perfumer called to Lily who quickly made a beeline towards her. A bottle of perfume containing the praises she had offered up to God, was poured over Lily. The Perfumer had captured the praise offerings and stored them in a rose-shaped pink diamond vial.

This was such a tender experience for Lily. She felt as if her heavenly Father had wrapped His arms around her in deep affection. She sat down to steady herself and bask in God's revealed presence. She could sense His pleasure which made her heart glad.

Sometime later Lily stood up. She was filled with God's Spirit and a unique, enthralling scent surrounded her. The Perfumer was sitting in a meadow just beyond her. Lily went and sat beside her, admiring the view. She then breathed in the fresh air and smiled.

"You are a picture of beauty, Lily," the Perfumer declared.

"Thank you Perfumer," Lily replied with a broader smile, "to be honest, I am awestruck at the beauty of this landscape."

"Yes, it *is* marvellous, like all the King's handiwork," the Perfumer acknowledged and then picked up her own special work of art and crowned Lily's brow with a dainty, grass garland dotted with tiny, yellow flowers. Beaming with pleasure, Lily hugged and kissed the Perfumer on the cheek.

"Is that a volcano up ahead? It seems to be smoking," Lily queried.

"That is our gentle giant, the Breather," the Perfumer informed Lily. "Actually it is breathing out white flowers not smoke. Baby's breath pours from its bosom and covers its summit like snow."

"Amazing," Lily replied.

"The wind also carries the flowers across the meadows and fields," the Perfumer joyfully stated as she pointed out the particular flower, "spreading the breath of heaven all around." The Perfumer directly turned to Lily and added, "It was once a violent volcano breathing out fire and brimstone." She waited for Lily's anticipated question.

"What happened to it?" came Lily's response.

"Its volatile activity caused the death of a baby whose family was picnicking in the meadow behind it. It is reported that the uncontrollable, anguished cries of the mother penetrated the hard stony heart of the volcano and was the catalyst in producing a heaving change of heart."

"Incredible!" Lily said staring at the mountain.

"But true, and from that day onwards the old nature had passed away and a new gentle nature filled the giant rock. The lava-filled valley was also transformed as you now can see."

"Goodness, that is extraordinary, even supernatural!" exclaimed Lily.

"Sure enough, the hand of the King brought this about and this specific area," the Perfumer pointed all around her then continued, "is specially guarded by the King's watchers."

Just then a fair lass about five years old approached the women. She had an enchanted air as if she had come from another world. In her hand she carried an open basket of flowers.

"That's Blanca," the Perfumer said to Lily.

"Is she a watcher?" Lily whispered overcome by the sacred environment.

"No, she is my sister," the Perfumer replied with exhilaration as she stood up.

"Good morning Perfumer and Lily," she greeted them with a smile and a hug. The women returned her greeting. Lily was fascinated at the girl's appearance. She was completely clothed in white.

In her pale-blonde hair was a band of white meadowsweet. Her knee-length tunic was comprised of white carnations, lilies of the valley, roses and fuchsias. Her feet were crisscrossed with pure white daisies which also formed a bracelet on her right wrist. In her basket were bundles of baby's breath and lilies of the valley.

"Before you leave I have a present for you," she said to Lily, motioning her to stoop down. This Lily did and Blanca added lily of the valley blooms to her garland. "There, it's looking like a tiara now," she declared contentedly. Lily graciously and gratefully kissed Blanca on the cheek.

"I could burst with happiness, you both have honoured me with your kindness." It was now time for Lily to continue her tour and she reluctantly said goodbye to her new found friend and acquaintance and prepared to move on. The Perfumer pressed a large white rose petal into Lily's hand and waved goodbye.

There was a message in navy ink on the petal that transferred to her hand - it read - 'The stare is in the stone.' Lily blinked and inhaled the sumptuous fragrance of the petal. The Holy Spirit then spoke to Lily reminding her of His faithful presence and encouraged her to resume her journey and converse with Him as she walked.

The weather on *The Narrow Trail* had up to this point been bright and sunny. Now there were more clouds and the sky had become grey. Lily also noticed that there were no more flowers in the meadows and that the trees were sparsely planted. The view was less appealing than the floral field and Lily was wishing she were travelling in the opposite direction.

Deep in her heart she was convicted of her need to trust the guidance of the Holy Spirit and to appreciate all the things He purposed for her life. Lily abruptly stopped as she observed a patch of dark, grey cloud that was moving towards her speedily.

It seemed very odd and before she could make up her mind what to do, she found herself encircled by locusts that were making quick work devouring her garland. Lily screamed, startled at the menacing swarm and tried to fend off their invasion. In a matter of seconds she was left bare-browed with sore hands.

Overwhelmed at her loss and the suddenness of it all, Lily started crying. She felt victimised and vulnerable again. She noticed that the meadows and few trees around were also completely bare.

"How long must I endure all this?" she cried out exasperated. "The bees were harmless, but scary nonetheless and these wretched plant-robbers...," her voice broke off as she tried to compose herself.

"You mean the locusts," the Comforter answered.

"Same difference!" Lily replied quite incensed.

The Comforter whispered words of reassurance to her hurting soul and urged her to take heart and continue the journey. Lily wiped away her tears, sniffed again and trudged along. There were no more junctions on the way, but now the path was leading downward into a valley. Lily felt very sad and yearned for something that would visibly lift her spirit.

"Sing," the Holy Spirit advised.

Just as Lily was getting ready to offer a sacrifice of praise, she spotted a colourful stand up ahead. Distracted by her desire for a change of scenery, Lily quickened her pace towards the site.

Coming closer, she saw it was a bargain booth, with a large sale sign in bold, red and white letters. Colourful banners fluttered in the gentle wind around the booth and a svelte, brown-eyed brunette wearing a V-necked, cerise silk gown with flowing sleeves was laying out eye-catching, gorgeous dresses of linen, silk, satin and rayon on the stand.

"My, what an interesting fragrance you're wearing," the seller of colourful garments commented.

Lily smiled, but couldn't help feeling self-conscious about her unsightly, plain rags. They had been bleached by the sun and as she gazed in the mirror beside the stall, she despised her threadbare look. Her hair was all tousled and it seemed that she was looking more and more like a drifter. She ached again for the loss of her garland.

"We swap old for new here, dear," the woman quipped, her glossy red lips widely parted revealing perfectly set, white teeth.

"Really?" Lily replied, relieved that the woman nodded as she had brought no money with her. The thieves would have taken it anyway. There were so many styles displayed that Lily wondered which particular dress to choose.

She picked out a striking cobalt-blue, linen dress and held it up in front of the mirror. What a difference it would make to her dull appearance, she thought. The inside label read Vanity Wear, one size fits all. Pricked in her conscience, Lily let the garment fall on the pile of other dresses. The price tag was £6.66.

"Don't be afraid to try something on. After all, you *need* a new outfit - you've practically worn that one out, haven't you dear," persuaded the seller.

"Think what it would do for your image?"

The war was on. Lily battled between her pride and her calling. She greatly desired to be rid of the rags, but the price required was not what she wanted to pay. As she wrestled with the lust of worldly things, she began to feel weak and dizzy.

Instantly she cried out, "Jesus, my King, help me!"

Lily leaned against a bare sycamore tree near the booth and her head began to clear. The seller stood carefully watching her while tapping her crimson-painted fingernails on the stand. The eyes of Lily's heart were opened to see the eyes of the black swan in the seller's face. A chill came over Lily as it seemed she was looking into the very eyes of the devil!

She then noticed that the sale receipts on the table were stamped 'Souled' instead of 'Sold'. The triangular, crystal pendant the seller wore at the end of a silver chain had taken on a hypnotic, bluish glow. Lily glanced at the faded message on her hand.

"You'll look charming in this," the seller suggested, holding up a shimmering, sapphire, silk dress as she flicked her straight hair. "Or this," she added pointing to a white, lace and satin evening dress.

"Charming?" responded Lily, who then recalled the scripture she had read in Proverbs: *'Charm is deceitful, beauty is vain, but a woman who fears the Lord will be praised.'*[28] Another verse came to her mind that said, *'what will a man give in exchange for his soul?'*[29]

The Comforter spoke and said to Lily, "You will either choose the glory of God or the glamour of this world. You cannot serve two masters."

Strengthened by His counsel, Lily resisted the temptation to exchange her eternal soul for the passing pleasures of the world and wisely hurried away from the *Booth of Bewitchment*, for that was what she realised it was.

"We'll meet again, Raggedy One," the seller called after Lily.

"I'm very glad I didn't lose you," Lily heard the Lord's words reiterate in her heart.

"Thank You Jesus, for providing a way of escape from the snares along my path and that Your word keeps me from sinning against You,"[30] replied Lily.

She continued on the trail, rejoicing in yet another victory over evil. Right there and then she purposed not to look with unholy longing at clothing or anything else.

The grey clouds had now been replaced by brilliant sunshine. Lily eventually approached a junction with confusing signs. *The Broad Way* lay directly in front of her on what was a narrow, dirt trail. The path signposted as *The Narrow Trail* was a perpendicular wide asphalt road, the sign had been twisted.

Suspicious of foul play, Lily decided to take the narrow path with the contrary sign. She placed her Bible at the foot of the sign, so that anyone who came behind her could see the path that she considered was right.

After walking two kilometres, Lily noticed that the trail began to widen into a desert and her feet were somehow sticking to the ground. Her throat was parched and her body felt baked by the sun. She had an impulse to turn around, but her feet were being pulled forward into what became a miry clay.

Distressed as to losing control of her direction, she cried out to the Comforter. Overwhelmed by the oppressive heat, Lily lifted a heavy foot and then her world faded to black as she fainted.

8

Double Crossing
"the shadows flee away" [31]

A tall, dark figure stood over Lily's fallen form. The sun was high in the sky and vapours rose from the steaming earth. Removing a helmet the figure released her pent-up, long auburn curls and flashed her emerald eyes sandwiched in thick eyelashes.

Stooping, she poured water from the cover of a black flask onto Lily's lips, then raised Lily's head and poured more water, this time into her mouth. With a swift move of her right hand she slapped Lily on the cheek and held her by her hair.

Lily stirred groggily, her face stinging, while her body lay like a log. Opening her eyes, a female face gradually materialised before her. The figure released its hold on her hair and Lily's head smote the ground. She groaned, blinked and tried to move, but felt completely drained.

"Get up, your nap time is over!" the figure yelled and then lifted Lily by her upper arms off the ground. Lily stood unsteadily, not sure if she was awake or asleep. The other woman was not amused at her condition in the least. She roughly splashed icy water on Lily's face.

Spluttering, Lily looked wide-eyed at the woman, while the icy water dripped off her chin, reviving her skin. "Can I have a drink?" Lily asked.

"That will have to wait!" the woman replied with ire, lifting the flask to her own head and drinking what water remained. She then shook her head and her hair shone as if on fire in the sun's rays.

Lily was not sure if it was the heat or not, but the woman looked exactly like her in features. She had a darker complexion, deeply tanned, thicker lashes and different colour hair and eyes. Her lips were dark purple, but everything else was similar. She was dressed in black - jumper, tunic, belt, leggings and sandals.

"How odd," Lily whispered looking at the stranger's attire and concerned at the anger in the woman's tone. "Who are you and why are you so angry?" she asked.

The woman's eyes narrowed to slits and turned to a murky green as she placed her left hand on her hip and spat her reply, "I am your nemesis, your lower self." She circled Lily and continued, "I have come to bring you to your senses, to.." she paused in front of Lily and said very slowly, "leave the muck and mire and find your true place at home."

"Home?" Lily queried, "Whatever do you mean?"

"Leave this godforsaken wilderness and go back to being your old self. I am tired of this journey; I can't breathe because of your ill-found faith. Stop this foolhardy mission and be who you once were."

Lily listened to her other self with empathy. She thought about her life before she met Christ. The emptiness of it loomed large in her mind as she recalled her flat at Manor Views. She once had a number of friends doing what *seemed* like fun, but deep down she wasn't really happy with her self.

No, she resolved, this was no time for turning back. But how could she go forward after presumptuously taking the wrong path? Lily sighed and silently asked the Comforter for help. He reminded her of the King's words and will for her life, to keep faith and continue the journey.

"I cannot go back, Nemesis," she declared.

"Then I will slay you in the desert," Nemesis concluded, extracting a small, black sword sheathed in her black, leather belt. Lily moved away while her eyes searched the desert floor. "You will find no weapon here," Nemesis ominously laughed as she donned her helmet and followed her prey.

"God, help me!" Lily cried to her Father.

"Use the Sword of the Spirit," was His urgent reply.

Lily dodged her nemesis' stabs, but in her weakened state fell prey to two jabs on her left shoulder and below her left rib cage, she then tripped over a small rock. Sweat oozed down her temples and her vision blurred.

From her spirit a scripture leaped to her mind and then her mouth, "No weapon formed against me shall prosper!"[32] A bolt of lightning followed her proclamation and struck her nemesis who was bent over Lily, ready to smite. A fierce look was etched on her face.

When Lily's vision cleared, she saw that Nemesis had become a white, stone statue - just as she was about to carry out her promise. God had saved her from a fatal strike. "Thank You Father," Lily breathed in relief. The spiritual sword had greater power.

As she scanned the scene around her, Lily noticed a huge rock to the east. Hopeful and keen to get into shade, she staggered towards it, leaving tiny drops of blood in her wake.

Leaning against the rock Lily pulled up short as she faced the other side. Someone was bent over a … a *river* of all things, in the desert! Somehow this did not compute. "I *am* dreaming," she muttered woozily to herself.

The river flowed from the north and came to an end a few metres in front of the rock with a pebble bank. An indigo carriage stood to the far left drawn by a grey donkey wearing a pink ribbon and a zebra with a red ribbon. The animals were refreshing themselves in the river.

The person straightened and turned around and looked directly at Lily, who drew a deep breath and froze in panic. "Do not be afraid," a gentle, masculine voice addressed her. "I am Favour, another friend of the King, please come and have a drink, I will bathe your wounds."

Lily stared at the faceless Favour who was dressed in a flowing, teal-hooded robe. His hands were also invisible, holding a beaker. She was so dehydrated that she was glad for the offer, though a bit wary, and like a parched, pained deer stepped towards Favour.

He met her at her first step, as he glided effortlessly in motion. Lily took the beaker and welcomed the liquid contents. Her throat was pleasantly soothed as she drank the fluid.

She handed him the empty cup which immediately refilled in his hand. He carefully tipped the medicine on her lesions. A burning sensation ran down her left side gently fading into a cooling tingle.

As Lily looked at the affected area she was heartened to find no tear, bloodstain or trace of any wound. *Miraculous*, she thought to herself.

She could sense that Favour was smiling at her even though she could not see his face. She smiled in return and said, "Thank you Favour. Do you mind if I wash a little?"

"You're welcome Lily, no I don't mind, dip three times and you will be all clean," he answered.

Lily stepped into the river and relished the smooth feel of the current on her feet. She followed Favour's instructions and immersed herself in the water three times. She regally rose from the river like a princess, sparkling in the sunlight and glistening with drops of water.

As she stepped onto the pebble bank and approached Favour, a warm wind wrapped around her from head to toe and in an instant Lily was completely dry. "That was *sooo* good," she remarked to Favour.

"You look wonderful. Now we," he pointed to the zebra and then the donkey and said, "Loving, Kindness and I must get you back to *The Narrow Trail*, you understand?"

Lily nodded and knew not to ask unnecessary questions from her previous encounter with the Perfumer. Favour climbed into the carriage and held the silver reins while Lily followed and sat behind him. He hummed a consoling tune as she rested her head and closed her eyes, thankful for the shade once again.

The sound of festive music wakened Lily from her doze as she opened her eyes to behold a bevy of maidens in joyful dance, holding tambourines with colourful streamers and wearing pastel costumes. A band of men dressed in shades of brown, were playing their pipes as they too joined in the merriment, interspersed among the women.

The carriage came to a stop and Lily was suddenly removed from her seat to find herself in the middle of the gaiety, dancing and laughing, as if with old friends.

When the music stopped, Lily was invited to sit at one of the rectangular, wooden tables that had been arranged for this party. Silver platters of cheese, grapes, apples, plums, roasted meats and fresh bread lined the tables with matching gravy boats, small bowls of honey and silver jugs of ginger wine. The menu was a welcome change to Lily. The chief minstrel, Vinnel, gave thanks and the feasting began with much jest and recitals.

Percy, one of triplets wearing a dark chocolate-coloured wig, stood up, cleared his throat and began, "I say, I say, I say," on the last two says, his brothers Wilkins and Mirth nodded in agreement. "Why was the carpenter invited to the wedding?" After looking around the expectant group, he disclosed with great pleasure: "To make sure the marriage would work, get it? Woodwork!"

Pointing to his wooden flute he then did a hop and a dance, spun around and with finger extended he nominated who should go next. A smiling petite maiden with long, plaited, white hair stood up and curtseyed. She then waved her tambourine in the air and sang a limerick in a beautiful soprano timbre:

"I greet you one and all
Glad news I have to share
I went to Marshmallow Street
My welcome there was oh so sweet
They proclaimed I was a ....dear."

"They proclaimed she was a dear!" the party replied as they clinked silver mugs in a toast. With a graceful twirl of her tambourine, the maiden selected a quaint-looking man sat on the bench across from her. It was Poddles! Aka the village clown; he donned his jester crown and stood. As he bowed his head, a green spotted frog leaped from the centre of his polka-dot crown and landed on the table. Its unexpected appearance caused quite a commotion which animated the amphibian even more.

It jumped on a maiden's head and then across the table to a platter of cheese, next to a piper's shoulder before hopping to the adjacent table. Covers clanked on the platters as a cacophony of shouts, screams and laughter sounded around the tables. Lily was beside herself with glee.

"Frog overboard!" cried a bemused piper as the creature landed in a pitcher of wine sending a huge spray of liquid upward.

"It's surely having a whale of a time," laughed a maiden.

"Frog flavoured wine, let's see," Tajio, a jovial piper stated as he raised the pitcher and took a whiff. "I think I'll pass," he decided as he set the jug down. Jumping wildly the frog eventually landed in an open bowl of coarse honey and found it quite difficult to liberate itself.

"How sweet," a maiden remarked.

"That's a sticky situation as I ever saw," expressed another.

"Anyone for honey-roast frog?" challenged an amused piper as he held up the bowl.

"I do fancy some spare rib-bits," joked another piper at the far end of the table as he rubbed his stomach.

"It's rabbits not ribbits that should come out of hats. This is most unusual," a senior piper enunciated while stroking his beard.

Up to this point Poddles had been busy whistling a tune and juggling apples and plums as he trotted in a circle around the group. However, the prospect of losing his miniature entertainer arrested his attention, so he promptly removed the struggling frog and berated it.

"You'll pop your clogs if you're not more careful!"

The amphibian jumped on his hat and Poddles smiled at his audience. He took a bow with a flourish while the frog stayed put which prompted their applause. Then he skipped and hopped and with a cock-eyed stare nominated Lily as his successor.

Lily participated telling a bit of her own story first, as her audience sat riveted. She decided on sharing a poem and taking a cue from Percy, cleared her throat to prepare.

"I turned my face to heaven
And closed my eyes to the sun
I opened my heart to my Maker
Now I'm having so much fun!"

"Now she's having so much fun!" they all affirmed with another toast. Lily pointed to a rotund lad at a far table.

"Okay," he said, "but I'll have to loosen up first." He got out of his seat and stretched upwards then downwards touching his toes. Simultaneously, a loud ripping sound was heard as the back seam in his trousers came undone. Howls of laughter echoed around the tables.

"Sounds loose to me," a piper concurred.

Highly embarrassed the lad turned a shade red and said, "Oh no! What a show, my pants have split. Oh woe! I've had too much food, it's not done me good, I can't let the missus know!"

"He can't let the missus know!" everyone sang and then got up laughing and held hands to form a circle. Around and around they danced and sang this happy song:

Laughter, that's what we're after
Laughter, the sound of joy
It's tonic for your soul
Age-defying
Let it take control
Of pain and sighing
Get a big dose
And you might be crying
Laughter, full of stitches
Laugh until you roll!

A sharp whistle interrupted the proceedings, signalling the end of the party. Lily searched the crowd for Favour and found him standing at the junction with the conflicting signs. He handed her the Bible she had left and bid her goodbye as she resumed her journey.

"Lord, thank You so much for rescuing, rejoicing and restoring me. I trusted my own understanding and went astray. I know I need to ask for Your direction and obey Your word. I will abide by Your truth."[33]

She opened the Bible and turned to the book of Proverbs. Her eyes rested on chapter 10 verse 29 - *'the way of the Lord is strength to the upright.'*

In response to the word Lily declared, "Keep me on Your narrow way Lord, strong and not fainting." She then took the wide, asphalt road grateful for another chance to complete her journey.

The road began to taper to a narrow track as she walked. *The Narrow Trail* no longer led downward, but straight ahead. Lily could see the road taking her to what appeared to be a dense forest. There was no way to bypass the forest without forsaking the path. "I must not walk by sight," Lily reminded herself.

She entered the forest and found herself in a dark, leafy world. The wind was very strong and carried her along the path, rustling through the oak trees with a sinister sound. Lily found it difficult to see where she was going as hardly any natural light was present.

What little light penetrated the forest cast eerie shadows around her. The sound of wild creatures filled her ears and Lily's heart skipped a beat. Was this her imagination or were there amber eyes peering at her from among the trees?

"O Lord, help me!" Lily cried in uncertain dread.

"Fear not," the Holy Spirit counselled Lily. "I am with you always."

Hearing His voice encouraged Lily and made her glad that she was not alone. The wind was blowing stronger and leaves were flying everywhere and Lily was not sure if she was seeing bats. She also wasn't sure if she was making the right turns among the trees.

Suddenly, Lily found herself sprawling, having fallen over a branch in the way. Her knee was bruised and she winced at the stinging pain. The Bible had fallen out of her hand and landed in a muddy swamp.

"If only I could see where I was going," she cried.

"My word is a lamp to your feet and light to your path, dear Lily,"[34] the Comforter compassionately advised. "Ask Me for direction, listen to Me and I will guide you through the dark."[35]

Lily stood up and wiped her chin and arms. Her rags were now wet with mud. "I'm not sure I'd like to see what I look like now; from clay to mud, what next?" she moaned. Remembering the Comforter's words and her own, she sought His guidance and was directed to turn left and so she continued her journey. Sometime later she stumbled and fell again, crying out in pain having sprained her ankle.

Attempting to move the stumbling block, Lily recoiled in shock as she realised that the obstacle was no broken bough, but a human skeleton! Immobilised with fright at the dim sight, Lily's heartbeat thundered in her ears. Callous fear craftily crept upon her, seeking to keep her bound on the ground.

Was this a graveyard? Could this place be the end of her journey? If so, rising from this fall was possibly impossible. Questions scurried through her troubled mind like rats. *Who had died here? How was she going to make it out?*

At that moment Lily suddenly found herself surrounded by thick black bamboo bars which stretched twelve feet high. Four feet above her head there were thick thorns on the bars that had the appearance of barbed wire.

The bars tapered into a cone shape forming the roof of this cage. Petrified and hardly breathing she silently cried out to the Comforter.

The Holy Spirit quickly brought comfort to her troubled heart and mind. He prompted her to recite Psalm 23 which Lily had committed to memory. When she got to verse four, *'though I walk through the valley of the shadow of death, I will fear no evil; for You are with me; Your rod and Your staff, they comfort me..,'* Lily repeated the verse until the fear was dismissed from her heart.

She stared curiously through the bars into the dark. On her knees, she went around the cage and felt each bar hoping to find a weakness, but they all were sturdy and solid like steel rods. This was no figment of her imagination.

A pale, crescent moon silently watched from above. The swirling wind blew leaves and dust into her face. Closing her eyes she asked the Holy Spirit what she should do next. She felt trapped, but not alone.

Her hands began to itch and in the dim light Lily could see the dark imprint of the bars she had touched on her fingers and palms. She wondered what the stain consisted of as a light-headed feeling came over her and she soon succumbed to the drowsy substance.

The gentle cooing of doves was the first sound she became aware of as she stirred out of her slumber. Dawn had painted the sky above - blue, pink and purple, providing more light through the dense foliage.

"Fiddlesticks! Fiddlesticks!" a voice cried in annoyance.

Lily opened her eyes and sat up as the words were repeated. Her eyes beheld a red squirrel who was a short distance away frantically digging around. Its eyes met hers and the animal stopped and scratched its head.

"What did you put on those sticks? I haven't slept this long in ages!" the squirrel queried.

"Good morning," Lily replied, "I'm not responsible for that as I too fell prey to the substance."

"Well how did you get in that contraption?"

Lily thought a bit then replied, "I was ensnared by my fears I think."

"Fiddlesticks!" the squirrel said again while scratching its head.

"My name's Lily, what's your name?"

"Isaac, but most folk call me Zak," the squirrel replied.

"Zak can you please get me out of here?"

"Can't say I can, besides I'm busy," and Zak resumed digging.

"What are you looking for?"

"This," Zak replied as he lifted a large pouch out of a hole. He opened it and pulled out a dried blackcurrant and some nuts.

"Food, oh good. May I have some Zak?"

Zak thought about it and then said, "Maybe," and swallowed a mouthful. The squirrel nibbled another nut and then rubbed its stomach and burped.

"Pardon me, one must not forget manners, 'specially in front of strangers."

Lily then cleared her throat and Zak ate another mouthful then approached Lily dragging the sack.

"You'll have to make do with this and I'll have to find another stash. The one I had last night was either stolen or blown away."

"Oh thank you Zak, there's enough in here and I am sorry for your loss," Lily remarked as she took the pouch.

Zak scampered to a nearby tree and began digging around it. In minutes he exclaimed, "Rats it's been stolen!" He then turned slowly around as if to spy out the perpetrator.

"Try somewhere else!" Lily encouraged as she partook of the currants and nuts.

Off Zak went and returned sometime later with a sack over his shoulder tied to a stick.

"Glad to see you found some," Lily declared.

"Indeed so am I, you find all sorts in this neck of the woods. One can't be too careful though, some creatures won't work for their food." He slowly scanned the area again and then said, "I didn't mean you by the way."

"No offence taken Zak," Lily stated.

"Good. Anyway, I must be off, the family's gathering and I'm behind time. Cheerio Lily!" and with that said, Zak scurried off to his appointment.

"Goodbye Zak, safe travels," Lily called after the hastily departing acquaintance.

"Holy Spirit will you help me, I can't journey into maturity if I'm shut in can I?" Lily asked

Only silence followed so she repeated the question louder this time. Again there was no response.

"Am I missing something here?" she cried in desperation.

The wind picked up again and dust and leaves swirled around her. Lily protected her eyes with her hand and heard a whisper in the wind.

"Mystery, embrace the mystery," the Holy Spirit counselled.

Lily considered His counsel and asked "Do You mean I'm not meant to understand my predicament?"

There was no response, so Lily spent the rest of the day pondering and praying for wisdom to discern when she would be able to move on. No other creature came her way and as night fell, she curled up and went to sleep. The Holy Spirit gave her assurance that He was with her even though she was still trapped and given no specific answer as to how and when she would get out.

The wind was blowing again when she awoke the next day.

"Deary me and to think that could have been me," a sympathetic voice spoke behind her, startling Lily. When she turned around, Lily saw the form of a fallow deer with what seemed to be multiple eyes instead of spots on its coat looking at her. At this point she did not know whether to speak or be still, but her curiosity got the better of her.

"Can you help me get out of here *please*?" Lily appealed with all her heart.

"That depends," replied the deer as its many eyes looked in different directions.

"On what?" Lily demanded Impatiently.

The animal started to pace and all its eyes fixed their attention upon her. Lily thought the creature to be quite creepy in a spooky kind of way. "That depends on how dear you consider your life to be," the deer replied quite soberly and before she could respond, it shook its antlers and said, "Not to you mind you, but to others."

"To others?" Lily queried and then thought upon the matter.

To whom was her life dear? To God, she thought, and Mrs. Hopkins, but no one else registered at that moment besides herself.

The deer addressed her again and said, "And if I told you that more troubles await you in the future that would make your present circumstances seem like a walk in the park, would you want to continue or simply stop trying and give up like so many have?"

The thought of more troubles was not very encouraging, Lily thought to herself and she wondered if the deer was trying her patience as a character test of some sort. She could easily say what sounded better if it would result in her freedom.

"My life is dear to others though they may be just few," she answered the first question.

"Yes and no," remarked the deer. "It is unwise to judge how many others you matter to, for you have no idea how much influence your life has had and will."

"No idea..." repeated Lily and at that instant the deer's eyes on its face and coat seemed to vanish to her astonishment. Lily peered intently at the deer in the faint morning light to be sure they were gone and not just shut. They had somehow disappeared.

"Indeed," said the deer, "without true vision you will perish, but you will succeed if you go the distance, finish your journey."

"How can I do that trapped in this cage?" Lily retorted.

Ignoring her manner, the deer gently advised, "Use the axe buried in the ground to cut the bars. Be careful not to cut your fingers on the axe as you extract it from the clustered, bamboo roots. Feel the numbers engraved on the rough axe face not the smooth. Divide the number into two and swing that many times on your left and to your right."

Lily found the heavy steel axe after painstakingly digging around her and felt the number twenty on the smooth side then twenty-four on the rough reverse of the axe head. "That's just a difference of four," she said to the deer.

"Yes and quite a difference," the deer asserted. "For without these four I would get nowhere," the deer said while lifting its legs.

Lily observed how majestic the deer's profile looked. She then breathed deeply and rose from the ground. It took much strength to rise from her fallen position.

"Farewell," said the deer and all its eyes returned and with simultaneous winks the deer disappeared.

Smiling while shaking her head, she decided to follow the creature's counsel and after eating the remnant in the sack, she hacked away to her left, reflecting on its words of wisdom. Each blow made a little dent in the strong bars. At the count of twelve the bars to her left remained in place and showed no sign of breaking.

Disappointed, breathless but determined, Lily turned her attention to the bars on the right which she attacked a dozen times. Weary and breathing very hard Lily dropped the axe on the ground and leaned on the bars in front of her. To her astonishment and relief they gave way as if they were made of tissue paper. Adding to her surprise was the fact that she hadn't used the axe on some of those bars.

"Thank You God, I know You will never fail me, the deer was right and I will always trust You and not give up. Continue to lead and guide me." Lily walked out of the cage, embracing her liberty. However, she now had a slower and an uneven gait.

"*Goodness and mercy shall follow me all my days,*" she continued to declare. As Lily said those words, she could hear footsteps behind her. She swung around to face a sight that brought any lurking fear to the forefront of her mind. A huge beast, like a grizzly bear was following her. It bellowed a frightful sound and then spoke.

"*Who* goes there?"

Lily was speechless. The beast was actually a huge gorilla with a crown of horns and sharp claws. Its eyes were a yellowish-green shade that had an ominous glow. The three horns that protruded from its head were white and the middle horn was the tallest.

"*Who* are *you*?" demanded the gigantic creature. The words 'who' and 'you' ricocheted off the trees and thundered in her ears. The gruesome sound echoed through the forest bouncing off more trees and Lily thought she could hear the cry of owls.

"I … I am a, a traveller," stammered Lily.

"A traveller?" the beast roared, "You are a homo sapien and *I* am your ancestor. The voice of your father speaks."

It was what the beast said last that strengthened Lily. After a quick prayer to her true Father, Lily responded.

"The voice of my Father indeed speaks and declares that I am a child of *God* not a beast. You are not my ancestor, never have been. I am created by God Almighty and so are you."

The beast laughed and then shook something in its hand that rattled then threw it at Lily's feet. She stiffened when she saw it was another skeleton.

"Who is this God? I am the spirit you have awakened with your axe. If you refuse to admit your evolution, you will end up like this!" the creature threatened Lily. The crown of horns turned red and appeared to be like burning coals.

"Father please help me," Lily prayed. All seemed silent except Lily's breathing as the two beings stared at each other. This was quite a contrast to the deer, but sure enough more trouble had come. It occurred to Lily that she might be required to lay her life down literally for Jesus. What *else* was out there drawn by her pounding the bars?

Then passages she had meditated on in Psalms and Proverbs flashed into her mind from her spirit.

The Lord shall preserve you from all evil, He shall preserve your soul, the Lord shall preserve your going out and your coming in from now till forevermore. Psalm 121:8

The fear of the Lord prolongs days; but the years of the wicked shall be shortened.
Proverbs 10:27

"Well - what do you choose - life or death?" the beast growled at Lily.

"I choose life - not by your hands, but by God - my Creator and Father," Lily said while trembling.

With vicious rage the dark creature with its outstretched ten claws rushed towards Lily who stood transfixed, again facing the threat of death. As soon as the beast came upon Lily, it disappeared and she realised that it was nothing but a shadow, an illusion, like a monster mirage. She let out a huge sigh of relief and amidst sobs thanked God for His protection.

She knew in her spirit that though she was weak in body, God had strengthened her to stand in faith and not bow to the beast's pressure. Lily leaned against a palm tree to steady her trembling legs and gradually slid down to a sitting position. She took a deep breath and looked around in the fading darkness and then was inspired to sing Psalm 27 as follows:

The Lord is my Light and my Salvation
My refuge in the dark,
When my enemies rise against me
When the path ahead I can't see,
The Lord is my Light and my Salvation
I will not fear for He is here
I will not fear for He is here.

When the wicked threaten cruelty
Speaking violence and blasphemy,
The Lord is my Light and my Salvation
In every situation,
He will not forsake me
I will trust for He is just
I will trust for He is just.

He hides me in His shelter
He lifts my heart and head,
Songs of salvation surround me
His goodness I believe to see,
The Lord is my Light and my Salvation
Each foe fails for Love prevails
Each foe fails for Love prevails.

The Lord is my Light and my Salvation
His Spirit is ever near,
Though my father and mother leave me
His faithfulness I will see,
His holy word upholds me
My heart is strong for to Him I belong
My heart is strong for to Him I belong.

In this posture, Lily was aware of a mighty covering that was over her. Her heartbeat had resumed its normal rhythm and a great calm had settled upon her. The Comforter then spoke and assured her that she was secure in the palm of His hands and living under His permanent shield - His presence and protection.

While holding the tree for support to stand, Lily noticed the skeleton too had disappeared and she was blessed with the sight of the sun streaming through a clearing up ahead. She could see it was her narrow way out of this forest. The light had cast shadows of palm tree branches like wings on the ground and as she passed the last tree, she read the sign attached to it, *The Forest of Shadows*.

Lily kicked away her flip-flops which were muddy, slippery, soggy and worn out. Thank You God," she continued, "Your goodness and mercy follow me all the days of my life. Anything else is a passing shadow and I will dwell in Your house, Your presence forever!"

Outside Lily was hit with a searing blast of heat as she came face to face with a blazing fire! Flabbergasted she took three steps backward to take in the alarming sight. "Oh no, not *another* trial!" she whimpered to herself.

A wooden footbridge lay ahead which was totally engulfed in orange and yellow flames. It seemed she had just been let out of the woods to face death by a foreboding fire. However Lily knew from her recent trials that things were not as they seemed.

She was feeling nauseous and thirsty from the heat and tempted to go back to the cool of *The Forest of Shadows*. But what delay or possible danger lay back there she did not want to know. Besides she was to go *through* the valley of the shadows not *stay* there. Turning back was not going to get her to the destination she was called to.

What was that destination anyway? A journey into maturity that lay only in taking *The Narrow Trail* she had been advised by the King. That was her special assignment.

"I must walk by faith not by sight," Lily again reminded herself. She resented not being able to relax for long and looked up hoping for a sign, but all was still. It was either progress through the fire or retreat in the darkness.

It was always a question of walking in darkness or in the light of God's word. Water oozed from Lily's pores as she made her decision. "My flip-flops," she moaned, regretting discarding them, though knowing they wouldn't be of much help, but possibly soften the impact. "God I'm miffed though I know I shouldn't be. You got me out of the forest safe and sound, but I could do with a hiatus You know. Anyway, thanks for Your help."

More silence followed. Lily looked at the fire and then sighed. "Holy Spirit, what will be my fate if I walk through the fire?" she asked.

In her heart she could hear His comforting voice reply, "You will be with the One who will never abandon you, I will accompany you all the way."

Lily swallowed hard and then gingerly took steps towards the inferno. Her body felt that it was already on fire before she placed her foot on the bridge. As she took one step after another, she was completely engulfed with flames.

Her eyes were closed and she felt intense heat, but strangely her skin had not melted nor was she burned. Yet she couldn't open her eyes and so she truly walked by faith across the bridge, one faltering step after another. Lily's right foot felt something hard and round and she realised that she had now crossed over on to a rough cobblestone path.

Opening her eyes she squinted in the sunlight and took a deep breath as she beheld a sight for sore eyes. A lovely winter scene lay ahead. Freshly fallen snow covered the ground and the evergreen trees lining the path. Her rags were still there and strangely not burned though she felt that they had been. Her feet welcomed the cooling effect of the snow and looking behind her Lily was filled with wonder.

The cobblestones she had walked on were sparkling with colour as they had been changed by the heat into gemstones and diffused with iridescent light. Behind that, the wooden bridge looked completely untouched as if there had been no fire near or on it! Like the beast, the fire had been a shadow of sorts. No wonder she was not to put her trust in what she could feel or see, Lily reasoned.

"How wonderful to be out in the open and in the light of day," she declared breathing in the fresh air. "Thank You God for keeping me on the right track."

She continued walking at a slow pace enjoying the snow-white scenery, the sunshine and the company of the Holy Spirit. Lily used some of the snow to wash the hardened mud off her face, arms, legs, feet, hands and hair. Though she rubbed hard the bamboo stains remained on her hands.

Looking down at her rags again, she noticed with sadness how terribly dirty they had become, quite ashen in colour. Better dirty than none, she observed in resignation. Her hair was worse for wear still caked in tufts of mud, but it would have to do. *The Narrow Trail* now snaked with many bends. Around the next corner Lily came upon what appeared to be a checkpoint.

A white stand was before her with two big-eyed, plain-looking female guards on either side. They wore white, skin caps which fastened under their chins, mocha brown feather tunics sporting a row of medals and flesh-tone leather, calf-length boots.

The sign above the checkpoint read 'Carry-On Crew'. There were stamped documents piled on the stand beneath a heart shaped onyx paperweight labelled 'Reports'. The guards smiled and the one positioned at the left spoke.

"Good day Lily, my name is Charlotte and my sister here is Sheryl. We are servants of the King."

"Good day," Lily returned the greeting.

"All travellers on this trail must produce passports to proceed," Sheryl added.

"But I was not provided with one!" Lily declared concerned.

"O dear that is unfortunate," Sheryl answered shaking her head and rolling her dark-brown eyes.

"Quite so," affirmed her sister with a nod.

"But the King did not mention this," Lily spoke up.

"Strange, it must have been an oversight," Charlotte claimed, placing a finger on her cheek.

"Judging from your bedraggled appearance, if you did have one it would not have passed inspection," Sheryl observed.

"I more than likely would have lost it by now," Lily admitted.

"There's only one thing to be done," Charlotte announced.

"What's that?" Lily asked as she watched Charlotte pull out a sheet of paper behind the stand and a feather from her tunic which she dipped in a bottle of ink.

"What baggage are you taking with you?" Charlotte asked.

"As you can see I have *none at all*," replied Lily a bit puzzled.

"Come, come now Lily, everyone has baggage of some sort," Sheryl asserted. "You know faults, issues, a chip on the shoulder and the like."

Charlotte nodded her head and added her own point. "You must confess your faults to us and," she paused for impact, "if you are honest, at the end the ink will remain black, if not it will turn crimson. Only honest confessions can carry on following the trail, you do understand?" Charlotte cautioned while Sheryl stared.

Lily nodded and started to think what her faults had been. The more she thought the sadder she felt and decided to share and get it over with.

"Well I have wandered off *The Narrow Trail* at times and got myself in bother."

"Yes, yes," Charlotte said eagerly.

"Details, Lily we need details." Sheryl reproved.

At length Lily stopped, quite perturbed by their probing and hunger for more. The page was now full and Charlotte waited two minutes, then lifted up the PASS stamp and pressed it on the document with satisfaction.

Sheryl lifted a brass tin onto the table. It had the word 'Meddles' engraved in black on the front. She handed Charlotte a gold medal and proudly pinned one on her own uniform.

"Carry on! You are *free* to go," Sheryl instructed with a broad grin as she put the tin away.

"This way," Charlotte indicated as she allowed Lily to pass.

"Thank you," Lily responded and walked on feeling uneasy and exposed, but glad to be on her way. Instead of feeling free she felt burdened. Looking over her shoulder she saw the two sisters studying the paper with great pleasure. She shook her head and decided to focus on the road ahead.

"I should have asked if they knew how much farther I needed to travel," Lily chided herself, but on reflection thought it didn't matter as they seemed more keen on extracting than providing information. They had not even detected details that were exaggerated.

It wasn't long before a brisk, chilling, northerly wind eventually began to blow and Lily hugged herself to keep warm. Compelled to keep moving and desiring to be out of the cold, she painfully quickened her pace.

On this part of the track there were a few centimetres of snow on the ground and what now lay before her were scanty leafless trees and bare, bramble bushes.

Suddenly, Lily felt a tap on her left shoulder and in an instant froze, not knowing if she should try to run or turn around. An ancient voice spoke.

"Excuse me, but I must have a word with you."

Turning around ever so slowly, she saw a snow-dusted tree trunk with a solemn face etched on its bark. A white, skinny leafless branch was outstretched in her direction.

"Yes?" Lily asked uneasily.

"Have you come this far by fate or by faith?"

"By faith," she responded. "Why do you want to know?"

The tree smiled and replied, "He who calls you is faithful to see you through. Let patience help you down life's road, no matter how long it takes to the journey's end."

"The sooner I get there, the better. I cannot dilly-dally, I must hurry on, it's cold," Lily grimaced, embracing herself.

"Yes, eager one, but see to it that you do not quit no matter *what* you face."

"Are you warning me about something?" Lily enquired with a tone of dread remembering the words of the deer.

"I'm an ancient voice in the wilderness, to call you to attention and to prepare you for your future."

"Humph," Lily remarked. "Anything else you'd like to advise?"

"Indeed. Take note, the wind blows but you must stand firm, though you get stripped like me. Having done all, as a traveller you must stand, rooted in God's love. The leaves may desert you, but God never will."

"Yes sir!" Lily saluted the tree and without further ado hastened down the soft white path. "A counselling tree, well I'll be stumped!" she chuckled to herself, "that's what I call barking mad or certainly going out on a limb. I hope he wasn't referring to more locusts. My, my, this journey is filled with all sorts of characters."

On approaching a bend in the road, Lily could make out what appeared to be a church building or some kind of chapel in the distance. She wondered what she would encounter next - friend or foe. Whatever the situation, she knew God would be with her.

9

The End in Sight

"Who is this coming up from the wilderness?" [36]

There were horses near the building's entrance. A white stallion stood out amongst the black, ivory and speckled ones. Suddenly, a black horse came whizzing by, its charcoal-suited rider shouted insults at Lily and hurled two eggs, disgusted with her state. Caught off guard, Lily had no time to duck and was an easy target.

Wiping her face and brushing off her sticky, wet, stained rags, Lily once again gave into feelings of not matching up. The rider dismounted and entered the building. Lily's thoughts were disturbed by another sound.

"Come, you are welcome," the voice boomed in her ear. "Your destiny is in this church."

Lily looked with longing at the striking edifice. A dèjá vu feeling swept over her. "Why do I believe that I belong there?" she said out loud.

"Because you do," said the voice closer, it was coming from the noble white steed that was approaching her.

"I can't go there like this, you saw what he did to me," Lily protested pointing at her dirty stained rags and unkempt appearance.

"You are forgetting your *true* identity - come, I'll carry you to the door."

Lily hesitated briefly before she mounted the stallion. Truth be told, she relished shelter from the biting cold and rest for her aching, tired feet. When she was seated, the stallion started to move towards the entrance.

The closer Lily came to the building, it looked to be even more beautiful. She admired the stately towering steeple, colourful stained glass windows and ornate stone work. The ivory horses were actually white, but paled before the brilliance of the majestic steed she was travelling on.

The horse brought her safely to the entrance. A shepherd leading his sheep through a gate was depicted on the window above the front door. As her feet touched the ground, the horse complimented her, saying "Your aroma is exceptional; what is it called?"

"I don't know," Lily responded, with surprise, thinking of the raw eggs. Then she realised that she indeed carried a beautiful fragrance. So turning to the horse she said, "I guess you could call it *Hallelujah.*"

"Yes, the perfume of God's praise, such a heavenly scent on earth. Cover your face, it will help you reach your destiny," the distinguished horse advised, pointing his dignified neck in the direction of the window sill, where lay an elasticised, eight-inch, grey veil.

"A veil! Why would I need that?" Lily said in surprise, then added, "oh, I get it, to mask my identity," once more revealing her desire to be hidden from view in her rags.

The veil was very tight-fitting and secure and only covered her face. The horse nodded then returned to the front waiting area where she had first spotted him. With veiled face, Lily peered inside the building. It was grander and larger than she had envisaged.

She saw row upon row of well-dressed people, a floral-lined very narrow aisle with burgundy carpet and a man dressed in white at the far front. She also noticed some seats at the separated back row where she could watch the event without being seen.

Apparently this was a wedding; the bride had not yet arrived. Lily shivered then looked at the sky and hoped that the bride would not get caught in the rain. Excited and eager to see the romantic event unfold, she selflessly stepped over the threshold and was confronted by a burly steward who seemed to appear from nowhere and pointed with scorn at her rags and bare feet and ordered her to get out.

The voice of her heavenly Father came strongly to her ear and He bid her not to fear, but to be bold and to believe that she could enter and find her place among the invited.

"Do not fear their faces," He instructed.

Trembling she took another step and determined to be faithful to her Father, so she moved past the steward of scorn and rejection and entered the church. Immediately, she experienced a mantle of peace and joy descend upon her. It felt so good to be here and indoors. Lily quickly seated herself at the rear. She noticed the scene on the last window to her right was of the prodigal son being embraced by his father.

A door opened to her far right and two men in smoky-grey suits appeared. The man in front had a Bible, Lily assumed he was the minister. He walked straight up to Lily and demanded that she vacate the chair for his own use. Shocked at his behaviour, Lily sat in quiet anger. After all there were a whole row of chairs beside hers that he could occupy. What *kind* of man was he? The other man behind turned towards her with a contorted expression on his face and barked, "What!" furious that she had chosen to remain.

Dismayed at the chauvinistic attitudes before her, Lily got up and quietly moved towards the vacant right row ahead of her. However, the silence was soon broken by the abrupt cries and shrieks from the left rows way ahead of her as these smartly attired guests stood and pointed in revulsion towards her.

Puzzlingly on the right, the guests there stood with welcoming smiles and expectant faces. Caught between the two, Lily froze and was tempted to flee. Her desire to be unnoticed by the waiting guests in front of her had just gone up in smoke.

Right then she heard a familiar voice bidding her to come. It was the King who had commissioned her, the Lord and Lover of her soul. It was *He* who was dressed at the front in white. He had commanded *her* to come to Him.

Amazed but encouraged, she looked at Him and took a step forward, then another. Her mind rationally argued against each step. She was aware of her ugly rags, shoeless feet and dishevelled hair. She did not appear to belong there, yet she had a contrary conviction that she was in the right place at the right time.

As she moved little by little, she could hear loud, scornful laughter from her left as the entire section conspired against her. To her right, she could make out loving words of support, as the gathered witnesses encouraged her.

Suddenly she fell to the floor, tripped by an adversary from the left. Her chin ached and her eyes smarted as she blinked back the tears, the scent of freesias wafted past her.

A man dressed in a black tailcoat jacket, white shirt, green tie, crimson waistcoat, pinstriped grey pants and black shoes stooped down beside her and said, "Still falling for me Lily?"

Sounds of hideous laughter filled her ears from the left. Lily stiffened as she recognised it was George's voice laced with sarcasm. She wondered how he had recognised her with the veil. He held her chin, but Lily refused to look at him by closing her eyes.

"You do know I have no interest in you whatsoever! I mean, look at you! If one can bear the sight!" He squeezed her veiled face then stood up and returned to his place.

More ridicule and scoffing filled her ears. On opening her eyes, a taunting face looked into hers and accused her of being a fool. Lily was startled to see that it was Charity! *Alive!* She was wearing an attractive, scarlet sequin dress, matching sling back shoes and her hair was beautifully styled in drop curls.

"Well, well, look who's here. Lily White or is it Tara Mud? What audacity to come in here like a *beggar!* You're not *fit* to show your face; do you think you will be accepted as you are in *your* filthy rags?"

More raucous laughter followed as Charity high-fived George and pranced to her seat. Humiliation flooded Lily's soul as she tried to get up. Through her tears she could barely see her Lord way up ahead looking in her direction. She felt ashamed because of the fall and her rags. The voice of her Lord came strongly again in her heart.

"Be strong and of good courage. Walk by faith and come. Lily, come unto Me and I will give you rest."[37]

"But my rags!" Lily protested, "I'm not worthy to come any closer."

"I have dressed you in My righteousness Lily, focus on Me, believe to see *My* goodness, press on, *do not* draw back!"[38]

With His uplifting words in her ear, Lily stood up and painfully advanced. In the fall, she had twisted her sprained left ankle. She could hear the babble of jeers and cheers around her. Each step demanded more strength and hope. She was limping now and had just stepped on a tack.

Seeking to avoid the obscure obstacles the left side had placed in the carpet, Lily fixed her eyes on the floor. The orange peonies and yellow freesias lining the aisle were trampled on the left. She would not be deterred Lily resolved in her heart.

"I must finish my course, my destiny is before me and I *will* reach it."

An old woman from the left, in a raspy voice cried at her, "Empty-handed, you are a selfish one. You dare to approach the altar with no gift? Do you not recall, it is more blessed to give than to receive?"[39]

Lily looked at her hands and thought to herself why she had come to a wedding without a gift, not even her Bible was with her.

"I lost it in the forest, but even if I had it with me it would be muddy just like my clothes," she whispered to herself.

Her Lover's voice broke through her troubled thoughts. "The sacrifice I desire is a broken and contrite heart. A humble soul I will not despise. So come, all I desire is your trusting heart Lily."[40]

A bouquet wrapped in grey paper was handed to her from the right. To her alarm, it contained only a mass of thorns that pierced her hand when she took it. The attached card read, *'through many tribulations we enter the kingdom. Acts 14:22'* Looking at the giver she was surprised to see it was none other than the STC messenger!

"There I was praying for good news," Lily scolded herself.

He wore a black tuxedo and bow tie, a white shirt and a wide grin. His eyes shone as he said, "I'm Mark and I'm on the right side Lily, my family too, because of your prayer and letter."

To say that Lily was knocked for six was very evident by the look on her face. The entire row smiled at her with grateful hearts. Lily smiled in return as she mentally processed this unpredictable turn of events.

She was now aware of a man in a midnight-blue suit with white shirt, striped tie and white handkerchief in his hand standing ahead of her in the aisle blocking her path. He sneezed and then screamed at her to leave and not sully the church, describing her presence as a mockery to the Groom.

Then he cried, "Lily, you are a thorn in God's side."

Lily looked at the thorny bouquet and the cut on her hand. She wasn't sure if there was a hidden message in all this. The man who was using her name, his voice was familiar. Whoever he was, she did not want to have anything to do with him.

"So you're a believer now. You're nothing but a traitor. How quickly you transfer your affections!"

He continued to glare at her menacingly. As he moved towards her she cried out, for just before her stood *Jim Preston!* Was this place haunted or was she hallucinating? Lily questioned herself again in astonishment.

A comforting hand touched her shoulder from the right and she was both surprised and reassured to see it belonged to none other than Mrs. Hopkins. Sydney stood beside her in a cream three-piece suit.

"Your perfume is lovely Lily," she complimented her friend.

Dressed in a duck egg blue linen dress with matching bolero and hat, she was elegant to behold. Whispering in Lily's ear she reminded her friend, "Many are the afflictions of the righteous Lily dear, but the Lord will deliver you out of them all."[41]

"Yes," Lily said suddenly calmed, "His grace is sufficient for me."[42]

"That's the spirit Lily," Sydney encouraged her with a thumbs up gesture.

Instantly a blazing light shone in front of Lily as the dove appeared and Jim fled to his place in the left row.

With a sigh of relief, Lily took another step and another. She was able to move without much interference it seemed and she was drawing nearer to the Groom. The notion crossed Lily's mind that she was possibly going to her judgement which would explain the presence of both the living and the dead.

The next person she encountered seemed to strengthen that notion as it was the apostle Peter. He wore an attractive robe and he gently touched her arm and admonished, "Be diligent to make your calling and election sure!" Lily nodded in response and then continued moving forward.

"Where is your wedding garment?"[43] a grotesque figure asked, peering up into Lily's face. It was the sneering midget! Confounded by the hideousness of this stylishly clothed man in a light grey three-piece suit, grey top hat and platform boots Lily turned her face away.

The question was repeated and she remembered that she had read that somewhere before. Yes, it was in the Bible. Jesus had judged that the one without a wedding garment was to be bound hand and foot and cast out of the wedding.

Lily looked at her rags and trembled. What did this mean? Immediately a verse came to her mind, 'Blessed are those who do not see and yet believe.'[44] Focusing on the Word, she declared, "My righteousness is of the Lord; He will perfect what concerns me."[45]

Each step of her broken march down the aisle, filled Lily with feelings of apprehension of what would happen next. Her heart thumped rapidly as she advanced.

An exceedingly handsome man from the left stepped in front of her. Lily was taken aback by his good looks. He wore a tailored white suit, peach tie and a red poppy corsage. He held her gaze with a grimace and sheer animosity towards Lily was mirrored in his eyes.

In a loud, intimidating voice he declared, "Are you not aware of your spots, wrinkles and blemishes?[46] The bride of Christ has none. Get out and get cleaned up, else you *will* face judgement. Isn't your God *a consuming fire*?"[47] He then held his head back and laughed with utter contempt for Lily.

His words sent Lily mentally reeling as she now realised that *she* was the awaited bride. That's why she was offered the veil!

"Of all the things, to be dressed like *this!*" she whispered frozen to the spot, forgetting her previous declaration. A torrent of thoughts washed over her. Who ever came to a wedding in such attire? A vagrant maybe, only to be driven out though.

The words of those who had previously chastised her, seemed to hold some truth. But the King Himself had called her to come. She wondered if this was a test. If she approached Him like this, would she be insulting or honouring Him? *What* was she to do?

Her mind went numb as a silent, internal debate ensued. It seemed she couldn't hear any reply.

"God *please* show me what to do, You know I never intended to cause a scene," Lily quietly uttered her desperate plea.

Was this a humility test? Just as she was about to turn around in confusion, a still small voice directed her.

"Press on, *do not* draw back!" came the divine summons again.

It was impossible for Lily to proceed until this obstacle had moved out of the way. His presence was not only imposing, but demeaning. He pointed at her and continued his derision.

"Have you not read in Proverbs that drowsiness will clothe a man with rags?"[48]

Lily looked away from him, desperately seeking a way forward. He peered into her face and said, "You know what that makes you? Sleeping Ugly!"

The whole left side exploded in unison, mocking and chanting the phrase in her ear. Lily closed her eyes and covered her ears. She did not want to see those wicked eyes again. Feeling woozy, Lily called for the Comforter's help. She couldn't focus properly.

In answer to her cry, God gave her a vision. Lily saw saints of old in a Roman arena, dressed in rags, being fed to lions, they were blood-stained but victorious. Reminders from Hebrews 11 regarding the trials of the faithful also came to her mind.

"Remember Vashti and remember Lot's wife!"[49] a cautious voice advised from the middle of the right camp. It was Mrs. Preston. Lily knew that the summons she had received was serious.

She then remembered the picture of the prodigal son's reception and thinking upon the courage of the saints who had gone before her, Lily declared in the power of the Holy Spirit, "If *God* be for me, who can be against me?"[50]

With those words the man vanished into thin air. Lily looked both astounded and relieved. She was almost at the end of her journey. The Bridegroom was just some yards ahead of her past the carpet.

A gentle-faced woman in a bright-yellow, georgette gown reached out to Lily, shaking her hand. It was Mrs. Atkins; her husband and Mrs. Spencer stood beside her. She lovingly cautioned, "Keep going, reach your goal, forget what's behind you and press on to the end. Possess your crown, your prize. Your Lord waits for you with open arms."[51]

In response to this exhortation, Lily proclaimed, "I must not draw back. I am my Beloved's and His desire is towards me."[52]

With the next step, Lily felt another hand, two this time, forcefully attacking her from behind and tearing at her rags. Yet another pair of hands held her arms. Lily screamed as she was knocked to the floor. Searing pain shot through her left foot which had been deliberately kicked and was now bleeding.

To her consternation she saw that she was being attacked by the very same thieves she had encountered on the broad trail! They were dressed in black suits and crocodile leather belts and studded boots. She tried to stop the attack, but realised that she had no strength left to resist these evil men.

In what seemed like seconds, she found herself almost stark naked before the whole assembly. Only the badly torn veil remained for which she was somewhat grateful to hide behind.

Lily could hear hysterical laughter and feel the mocking, lustful eyes of those from the left. Never had she felt so mortified and petrified; she was naked and deeply ashamed.

"No, not *now*," she whimpered, crouching in shame and agony, attempting to shield herself from the unwelcome gaze of the onlookers. The temptation to flee rose up inside her again, but was stymied as she could not bring herself to turn around and face everyone. Besides, it was such a long way to go.

Her heart and her feet ached badly and the narrow aisle seemed more like a runway. This was one flight she would have to miss. A sense of destiny and the memory of Nemesis cautioned Lily to stay put, progress and finish her assignment. Besides, the King did say that it mattered.

Thinking that she had terribly failed her Lord and King, Lily dared not look in front of her. So instead she stared at the floor. Her body felt cold on the bare surface. A twisted, taunting voice lashed out at her.

"You lily-livered soul! You didn't buy your white garment and now the shame of your nakedness is revealed."[53]

It was the garment seller who was now gloating in Lily's shame. She wore a purple linen dress with pearl trim, a red scarf and red stiletto heel shoes embellished with topaz stones. Her glossy scarlet lips were pursed together with satisfaction.

Lily could remember reading the verse, "Behold I am coming like a thief. Blessed is he who watches and keeps his garments, lest he walk naked and they see his shame."[54]

She had tried to be watchful, but not enough it appeared. Circumstances as they were, had gotten way out of her control. What *could* she do? The word of the ancient tree came back to her mind just then, "You must stand firm though you get stripped like me, having done all as a traveller you *must* stand."

How *could* she stand beside her Lord in *this* condition? Lily objected. She now had no clothes, no dignity and no apparent hope.

"Didn't I tell you, you would end up with *nothing? NOTHING!*" the reprimand came from Charity who had come behind Lily.

"You are a bigger fool than I thought you were."

Charity then ripped off the torn veil from Lily's face and strutted away triumphantly.

Lily was heartbroken. Her forehead throbbed with pain. Undoubtedly, this was the last straw. She couldn't bear life anymore. She wanted the ground to just open up and take her away.

Surely the Lord couldn't want her now. No one could. Just look at me, she reasoned, bowed over and feeling completely gutted. It was one thing to believe His counsel dressed in something, but in *nothing at all?*

Suddenly the floor before her began to split in multiple directions and right in front of Lily's downcast head sprung up a six inch, pale yellow root with a very woebegone form. In dreadful animated fashion it began to wail, "Woe is me! Woe is me!"

Mystified at this development, Lily stared stupefied at the plant. Its guttural groan was accompanied with an infectious, depressing mood. Unable to bear this mournful drone any longer, Lily grabbed the root by the neck and began to pull it up. The more she pulled it, the sound dwindled.

Determined to be done with it, she exerted what little strength remained and fully extracted the growth and threw it behind her. Weary and weak, Lily laid her head on her crossed arms resting on the wooden floor and began to cry.

"Whose *fault* is this now?" a stern, sarcastic voice asked while gawking at Lily kneeling right in front of her.

Lily reluctantly raised her head to find Sheryl staring at her once again. She was wearing a sleeveless, jade satin maxi dress and a white feather on her skin cap with matching elbow-length, satin gloves, a medal charm bracelet circled her left gloved wrist. Sheryl sneered and then was pushed aside by Charlotte who approached from the right.

"Quiet sister! She's suffered enough!" Charlotte asserted and then looked kindly at Lily and said, "Lily I am so sorry. We weren't doing the King's business at all, but picking at your past, at dead works of the flesh. We took advantage of you just as those thieves and gloried in your shame. Please forgive me for the gossip I passed on about you."

She took a deep breath and continued, "It's *our* deeds that were shameful, preying on you instead of praying for you. I have repented for meddling into matters best left unknown and for wronging so many people." Tears trickled down her cheeks and on to her white satin shift dress.

Lily looked sadly at Charlotte whose countenance was softer without the skin cap. Her shoulder length, golden-brown hair was flipped at the ends and she almost seemed angelic. Lily nodded her forgiveness and Charlotte softly squeezed Lily's right hand then placed a thick catalogue she had kept behind her back into Lily's lap and returned to her seat.

A picture of Lily from the Garden of Freedom was on the cover of the catalogue which had the words 'Lily's Errors' in bold blue letters on the front. With a painful sigh, Lily turned the catalogue over and placed it on the floor beside her. The words 'Amalek Press' were printed at the bottom. Still feeling wounded and exposed, Lily bowed her head.

"My child, look here!" a rough, manly voice demanded.

In deep sorrow, Lily looked around to her left and saw her father in a maroon suit standing beside her mother dressed in a matching gown on the far left of the front row. Their eyes met in a pool of love, concern and pent-up grief.

"Dad! Mum!" Lily croaked with a huge lump in her throat. Tears fell like a fountain from her eyes as she looked at them.

"Curse God and take this shawl to cover yourself; the man up *there* means you no good, even his *servants* are rotten. Let me comfort you Lily," Mrs. White appealed to her daughter.

"Curse God Mum?" Lily shook her head and sobbed, "No I cannot, I cannot! I missed you both *so* much."

"Come to us Lily," her father commanded. "He only wants to humiliate you further, he's obsessed with that kind of thing. Don't give him another chance Lily!"

The call of her own flesh versus the Spirit had Lily's soul in a tug of war. She desperately wanted to be with her parents and was losing sight of her Lord. The shawl would provide the cover she so crucially longed for and she surely couldn't endure more suffering.

"Lily, look at Me!" her Lover's voice replied in her heart, shaking her out of her turmoil, "I *hate* separation!! Draw near to *Me*, for with God all things are possible."[55]

Then she heard these words, "Rise up, My love, My fair one and come away."[56] The voice of her Lover came soothingly to her despondent heart. "I resist the proud, but to the *humble* I give grace. Lily you are fellowshipping with My sufferings. Don't forget, I too was naked before a crowd. I didn't try to save Myself. Follow Me Lily. Remember I created you. If you suffer with Me, you *will* reign with Me. Come forth My beloved, endure the cross and despise the shame. Rise again, I did, you can too."[57]

"Ha! Didn't I tell you? He wants to nail you to the altar right in front of everyone. Resist him Lily, he's got two Marys and John ready to watch you!" her father pleaded.

Lily quickly glanced at the altar and saw three other people through her tears. She turned away and was not sure what to think as doubts were creeping into her mind about her Lord's motives. Was more humiliation His path to humility? Would He actually nail me down? She remembered that He was a carpenter and shuddered.

"Lily, look at Me!" her Lord reiterated, "If you trust Me you will see My goodness. I cannot deceive you because I am the Truth!"

The mocking became less audible to her as she listened to the Lover of her soul. His words cleared the fog in her mind and provided a way of escape from the temptation to desert Him. He began to sing, lovingly disarming her fears:

Arise and come away with Me,
To a place of intimacy Lily
A place of pure transparency,
You'll see there's no need to hide,
I have chosen you as My bride,
There's no need for you to fear,
For I have led you here,
Arise Lily and come away with Me.

An unexpected desire to laugh welled up within her. Then in faith, Lily turned, fully raised her head and looked at Him. She wiped her tears and saw that He was looking at her with deep kindness and love. She smiled in response and then recognized the three people standing alongside Him. To the left was the Perfumer and Beth. It was somewhat comforting to see more of her friends here. To the right she could see a man that she recognised from his head and stature as the minister at Jim's funeral. Their backs were towards her.

She recalled that Jesus's close friends were at His crucifixion and wondered if she was really going to die first and then see His goodness. An altar boy appeared dressed in black and white with a white unlit candle in his hand. Lily intuitively recognised him as Isaac, the son of Abraham. He smiled at Jesus and then stood beside the minister.

"Though I'm down, I'm not out. I've got a bright future ahead of me. Finish the journey." The words of the cheerful caterpillar and insightful deer came back to Lily and her Lord's words, "I didn't try to save Myself. Follow Me Lily. If you suffer with Me, you *will* reign with Me."

Words of encouragement from Romans 8, were now dancing in her heart as the Comforter reminded her:

There is therefore now no condemnation to those who are in Christ Jesus, who do not walk according to the flesh, but according to the Spirit...Who shall separate us from the love of Christ? Shall tribulation, or distress, or persecution, or famine, or nakedness, or peril, or sword? As it is written: "For Your sake we are killed all day long, we are accounted as sheep for slaughter."
Yet in all these things we are more than conquerors through Him who loved us.[35-39]

"Rooted in God and trusting in His everlasting love *not rejection*, I am more than a conqueror; God is for me not against me, I will not fear," Lily whispered as she reflected on the ancient tree again, Isaac's appearance and her Lord's song. In response to an irrepressible urge to shout, she testified out loud, "I *am* more than a conqueror through Christ!"

The building was curiously quiet after her declaration. Shock waves went through the left camp as they reeled from her revelation, silencing their mockery.

"Well done, Lily!" resounded her Lord's approval. "The truth has made you free from the chains of shame, deception and fear."[58]

Indeed Lily felt the emotional chains that were around her soul had been shattered with her earnest confession. Once again the spiritual sword had cut off the lies. Peace now engulfed her.

"Tell Me Lily, what did you see on your right?"

"The congregation of the righteous," Lily replied after some thought.

"And to your left?"

"The assembly of the ungodly," Lily answered.

"You answer well; now Lily, tell Me, where is your wedding garment?"

His voice was gentle, but firm and Lily was at first surprised by His question. He wore a three-piece white suit, notched lapel, white tie, shirt and shoes and looked handsome and immaculate head to toe. What a contrast to her own lack of attire, Lily thought at that moment.

However, reflecting on His words, she recalled that He was referring to her right standing with Him. Placing her faith in His word, she replied, "It's the invisible robe that You have put upon me Lord."

"Quite right! Should you have been listening to the counsel of the ungodly?"

"No Lord, at times I was foolishly tossed to and fro by their twisted words."[59]

"What happens to the ungodly in Psalm 1, Lily?"

Thinking back to what she had read, she replied, "They are like the chaff which the wind blows away."[v4]

"So be it," her Lord announced.

Suddenly a twister enveloped the left section muffling the curses and screams that the damned were uttering. It picked up the shredded rags, veil and the root of rejection on the carpet and like a rope wound it around the cursing throng.

The next moment the floor opened beneath them and they descended to await their judgement wrapped in the whirlwind. Lily was totally unaware of what had occurred behind her.

"God is not mocked Lily, what one sows, one will reap. You are part of My harvest, good fruit that will remain to the end. Your faith is precious to Me; I am highly pleased with you."[60]

She remembered that the Lord was looking at her heart and not her appearance, just as the minister had said. Yes, His focus was on the invisible not externals. It was *all* about her heart.

"Lily in your letter to Charity you stated that you'd rather have Me and nothing else. Is that still true?"

The question searched Lily's soul and she contemplated her answer then said, "I uhm, yes Lord it is, though I found it very difficult, even stressful, to deal with my nakedness. But now I know that it's not what I've been through or what I have or don't have materially or physically or even intellectually that gives me dignity... or makes me acceptable and complete as a person, it is You."

Her response was deeply gratifying to the King and He tenderly advised, "Whatever you face, be assured that My love and kindness will never leave you. Be at peace, knowing that I will work *everything* to your advantage.[61] He then gently asked, "When I look at you Lily, do you know what I see?"

Lily shook her head as she awaited His answer.

"I see you as My treasure, one whose heart is truly devoted to Me; one who is learning to rise from every fall, to look at Me and stand tall, to trust and obey and live in My glory, in My righteousness – in My unshakeable kingdom! Your faith is very precious to Me. I love you Lily."

Lily's eyes filled with tears and He continued, "As you trust and obey Me, I am perfecting your soul. Adam and his descendants know only too well how to fall. As My new creation Lily, you have My nature, the capacity to rise again and win. I rejoice to finish the good work I began in you. To complete it Lily, not terminate it. You are a significant part of Me, part of My body, I cherish You." He was smiling at her, His hand reaching out.

It was only then that Lily took note of the beautiful scenes on the two high windows in front of the altar. One was of Jesus' hands washing a disciple's foot and the other of His hand helping a woman rise from the dust.

To meet Him she would choose to finish her course, to walk *by faith* and not by sight Lily reminded herself, dressed in His righteousness alone.

"You arise as the dawn. You are pure as the sun, fair as the moon," then smelling her fragrance He added, "and utterly captivating."[62]

Hearing her Lord speak these words, Lily arose. She winced as pain shot through her feet again. However, her mind and heart were focused on the one she loved above all else, who had called her to Himself. So looking unto Jesus, Lily smiled and decided that she would remain standing. She then boldly took the final sacrificial steps towards His presence.

10

Transfigured
"O prince's daughter!" [63]

As Lily touched the Groom's hand and stood by His side at the altar, she heard her Lover say, "You are beautiful My love, there is no spot in you."[64]

To her increasing joy she no longer felt ashamed; she was covered in a new dimension of His glory. She now understood the purity that Adam and Eve walked in before they sinned. It was the very righteousness Jesus had imparted to her spirit that permitted her to stand in His presence blameless. Though she had not always acted righteous, it was now crystal clear that was who she *really* was in Christ. A partaker of His divine nature.

Then He said, "Behold, you are fair My love! Behold, you are fair! You have dove's eyes behind your veil."[65] He lifted the veil of her natural eyes by His word, so that she could see supernaturally, in the realm of the spirit, His righteousness shining upon her just as she had seen in the River of Life.

All sense of nakedness had forsaken her and Lily perceived that the glory/righteousness of God which clothed her transcended anything fashionable on the catwalk or high street. She felt regal and complete to her very bones.

She was then miraculously covered with a radiance that transformed her robe of righteousness into a glorious bridal gown of celestial, fine linen, now visible in the natural realm.

Lily felt wondrously clean; her hair and her skin were glowing. All pain, blood, stains and bruises were in an instant, gone. Her feet were dressed in stylish, lace sandals. Lily could see the awesome glory of the Lord like never before.

The Perfumer was covered in blossoms and blooms of every shade of pink. She turned and dressed Lily's hair in a lovely pattern with different sized white blooms then lovingly announced, "The King greatly desires your beauty: for He is your Lord, worship Him."[66]

In humble response, Lily knelt before Jesus and while looking into His eyes, she began to sing with elation:

Words can't express Your loveliness,
Words can't express Your worth,
I try my best, but I must confess,
Words can't express Your worth.

With her face aglow she continued in praise:

More beautiful than a baby's smile,
More beautiful than a loving child,
No bride in wedding gown,
No monarchy in crown,
Can compare with the beauty that You are.

Lord, You are beautiful,
Your face, Your name, Your ways,
So beautiful, so beautiful,
Such majesty I find,
Enrapturing my mind,
My Bridegroom, Lord and Friend
My reverence has no end,
As I behold the beauty that You are.

More beautiful than a fresh bouquet,
More beautiful than a summer day,
No artist can portray,
No created tongue can say,
The fullness of the beauty that You are.

"I love and adore You Jesus," Lily certified in absolute bliss.

Beth, dressed in a flowing peach bridesmaid gown, presented a crystal case to the Bridegroom. He opened the case and placed a jewelled, gold crown upon Lily's head and lifted her left hand to put a sparkling, diamond ring on her finger. He then triumphantly declared, "You have known affection, affliction and rejection by many, now you know perfection by Me. I hereby crown you with everlasting peace, glory and double honour. Enter into the *joy* of your Lord!"[67]

With that declaration, He lifted her up by her hand and kissed her forehead. This was followed by thunderous applause and shouts of joy from the guests.

The Perfumer held out a scented, burgundy robe with a golden, brocade lining to the King while the minister also presented on a similar colour, velvet cushion the Sovereign crown. The King adorned with these emblems, then decreed, "Behold I make *all* things new."[68]

Lily felt a warm surge of divine electricity flow from her head to her feet. She knew that He had sealed a new name upon her. Then in harmonious symphony the witnesses sang:

The Lord God omnipotent reigns!
Let us be glad and rejoice and give honour
to Him,
For the marriage of the Lamb is come
And His wife has made herself ready.[69]

The atmosphere was saturated with the fragrance of worship. The Bridegroom announced to His bride, "A new city awaits you My love, the New Jerusalem." He then laughed in victory and Lily filled with exceeding ecstasy, joined Him as He stepped towards the aisle. He was now dressed in a regal white robe and gold cummerbund.

When she turned around to face the guests, she found to her astonishment and delight that the former left rows were completely deserted including the crushed flowers. She noted too the rags, root and torn veil were all gone.

The passage at the end of 1 Corinthians, chapter 1 came clearly to her mind.

"Yes, indeed," she whispered in her Lord's ear, "You do choose the weak, base and despised things to bring to nothing the things that are esteemed by men, to *Your* glory alone."[v27-29]

Majestically He confirmed, "My people shall never be left in shame - I've personally paid the price to secure that! Bring the catalogue to Me Lily."[70] Lily retrieved the thick book off the broken wooden floor and brought it to her Lord who then instructed her to flick through it.

Lily quickly scanned the pages which were filled with accounts of wrong deeds that she no longer recalled. As she closed the book her Lord declared, "It's time to set that record straight."

The minister was smartly dressed in a greyish-green jacket with peaked lapel, grey waistcoat and trousers, white shirt, patterned tie and green shoes. A worthy best man, Lily concluded. He smiled at Lily and held out an open half-filled, octagonal, garnet bottle with red correction fluid to Lily and said, "This is the blood of Christ, pour it on the log."

As she poured, the liquid penetrated the thick cover of the catalogue, leaving the cover dry and intact. Lily looked up at the Lord who smiled and said, "Review the pages." This she did, after giving the empty bottle to the minister, and was thrilled to see that the accounts were all blotted out, leaving only blank pages.

Isaac passed the candle to the Perfumer who then handed her a lilac scented white candle and instructed her to hold it up to the Lord's left eye. As Lily did so the candle was lit with a fiery, blue flame.

"Place the catalogue on the altar and burn it," the Lord commanded.

Lily obeyed and put the voided catalogue of errors on the silver altar before them. It ignited with a whooshing sound and soon became a heap of white ashes.

The minister then said, "This represents Christ's broken body," as he handed her a heart-shaped, large, mauve magnet with a jagged rift in the middle.

Lily placed the candle on the altar then took the divided object and held it as a whole unit as she passed it over the ashes collecting them all in one swoop.

"Ashes to ashes, dust to dust, find your place beneath the earth's crust," the King declared.

The split floor opened up wider before Lily's feet and she carefully dropped the magnet into the gap which closed after receiving the elements.

"There, done and dusted. No more bad reports!" the King said to Lily with a glorious smile.

There was a faint tremor underground and the wooden floor was fully restored to wholeness. Lily felt a gentle balm bathing her mind. At that moment a strong sense of union with the Lord filled her.

She was acutely aware that at the cross Christ had made an end of her sins, by taking them *all* on Himself. He had poured out His life to *make and keep* her new. Righteous forever. He deeply loved her and had paid the ultimate price for her to intimately know His glory; to transfigure her into a righteous heir, royal and *red*eemed.

It was the stately duty of every such heir to obey and honour Him, to remember the blood, meditate on the good, to have His mind and so be confident in His presence.

"Lily, now you see afresh the power in My blood. The moment you repent, the record against you is immediately erased. It's a blank page. Whenever you turn to Me, you turn away from sin and its hold on you. You have My mindset which blanks out those forgiven deeds. I deem you to be totally innocent, unblemished, untarnished and undefiled. Just as I originally intended."

His eyes shone as He continued, "Anyone who chooses to mention those deeds to Me again will be in contempt of My righteousness. You are gloriously redeemed. Utterly justified. From now on you will take stock of the praiseworthy aspects of your life with regular inventory."

Looking deep into her eyes He laughed heartily, releasing a wave of joy that flooded Lily's soul as she joined Him. He then turned her around once more to their waiting audience.

Standing at the end of the carpet was Blanca with her basket of flowers. A long column of baby's breath had replaced the crushed flowers that once lined the former left row. Blanca stepped forward, curtseyed and said, "Congratulations!" as she shook the hands of the bride and Groom. She then joined her sister and Beth standing to the side.

The remaining guests appeared to be shining like beautiful ornaments, chosen precious gems congregated before Lily. Representatives from every clan, country and continent were present. She knew that they were her family in Christ, those who had travelled ahead of her. She could also see numerous angels in the room, some were standing, others were in the air, engrossed in the blessed event.

The stained glass window to her right was aglow with light and showed a field of white flowers with the caption 'Consider the lilies.' A radiant young woman stepped towards Lily.

"I'm Jessica Johns. I believe you dropped this," she said, handing Lily the bouquet that had fallen out of her hand.

It was now filled with aromatic, white calla lilies and freesias, pink and peach peonies, wisteria, eucalyptus, glowing sprigs of baby's breath and lilies of the valley all tied with a pea-green silk ribbon. Lily thanked her and then looked across at the Perfumer and Blanca with a grateful smile.

Beth warmly hugged Lily and offered her congratulations. Her hair was styled to perfection with miniature yellow blooms and her countenance radiated with utter joy.

"Beth, I'm so glad to see you. I saw your parents earlier."

"I couldn't miss this opportunity Lily, neither could they."

"I'm honoured to have you as my bridesmaid. You are a great blessing to me," Lily stated with deep appreciation.

Looking very distinguished, a well-groomed man came forward and kissed Lily's free hand with a satisfied smile. Lily recognised him as Mr. Dean and returned his smile with a genial, "Thank you."

As he moved to the side, a notable woman took his place. She wore an opulent, white velvet hooded cloak, fastened at the neck with a mother of pearl, heart-shaped button. In her hands was an impressive amber treasure trove intricately embroidered with delicate pearls. She bowed and with a heartfelt smile introduced herself.

"I am Carlotta, a Guardian of the Pearls. You knew me as..."

Lily gasped at Carlotta's breathtaking beauty and said, "Charlotte!" in unison with Carlotta. Carlotta then opened the lid and revealed its contents. Lily gasped again as she saw the finest array of pearls displayed on a lining of mint green velvet.

Gracefully, Carlotta fitted Lily with pearl drop earrings, a matching necklace and then lifted up a three tiered bracelet and fitted it on Lily's right wrist.

"There you are Lily," she said with delight, "pearls are to be safeguarded not trampled. Therefore, only those who are worthy of keeping them with the utmost care should have access to such personal items." Her eyes shone with humble joy as she beheld the bride and Groom.

Lily was deeply moved by this gesture and joyful tears filled her eyes. She kissed Carlotta on the cheek and said, "You are a wonderful example of God's grace. Thank you Carlotta, this means a lot to me."

Up the aisle, she was thronged about by the remaining witnesses all now similarly clothed in fine, white linen. They rejoiced with her and the Lamb, her saviour, husband and Lord. The wondrous picture of two angels, Goodness and Mercy, raising glasses in a toast with confetti falling around them, portrayed on the window to her right near the entrance, caught Lily's attention.

"I'll drink to that," she said in evaluation as she thought of herself and her spiritual siblings, especially Mark the STC messenger. She was surrounded by hearts, hands and words of love. Lily's heart overflowed with gratitude and joy.

In adoring praise Lily professed, "I will greatly rejoice in the Lord; my soul rejoices in my God; for He has clothed me with the garments of salvation; He has covered me with the robe of righteousness as a bridegroom decks himself with ornaments and as a bride adorns herself with jewels."[71]

At the doorway, two tall men humbly bowed before her and each said, "Your Grace."

The one without the Bible declared, "Indeed the Lord has made you the capstone."

The other man added, "This is marvellous in our eyes."

Lily nodded with a kind smile, humbly acknowledging the weight of her crown. Outside the sky was azure and cloudless. Trees and bushes were budding and birds were hopping among them.

Jesus looked at Lily and said, "Rise up My love, My fair one and come away. For, behold, the winter is past, the rain is over and gone. The flowers appear on the earth; the time of the singing of the birds has come, and the voice of the turtle dove is heard in our land. The fig tree puts forth and ripens her green figs and the vines are in blossom and give forth their fragrance."[72]

His smile dwarfed the sun and wrapped Lily in its brightness. To say that she was captivated by His countenance was a colossal understatement.

Not a single black or speckled horse remained outside. He helped His bride mount His waiting white steed as He again called her to arise and come away. Then holding His robe He gallantly mounted the splendid stallion while bidding the guests farewell. Riding in His loving embrace, Lily experienced unspeakable pleasure enveloped in His glory.

Her name was whispered on the wind and she turned around to see a large cherry tree with a happy, blooming face that she recognised at once. The tree was robed in glistening, swaying, white blossoms that moved Lily's heart wonderfully. Zak suddenly appeared poking his head out of some blossoms and saluted. Lily laughed at the cute sight.

A handsome, chestnut deer stood beside the tree with smiling eyes, waving its antlers. She waved her regards to the tree, Zak and the deer, then looked up to see the words Bee-utiful formed above her by none other than the singing bees. They too were rejoicing and soon busily buzzed away.

An exquisite butterfly flitted past her and proclaimed, "Remember me? I told you I had hope of a better future. I too am a new creation, no longer a crawling caterpillar, because old things are passed away and behold all things are new."[73]

Another striking butterfly appeared and declared, "I've experienced a second birth and risen to new heights, dressed in dazzling splendour."

The transformed creatures then winged their way onward. Lily watched them fly away and noticed that her Lord was enjoying her fascination. They rode through an orchard filled with trees that were laden with pleasant fruits. The aroma of spices flavoured the air.

Lily took a closer look at the resplendent ring adorning her finger and gasped in immortal amazement as she saw her reflection, it was the same glorious face she had beheld in the mirror of the Bible.

"The stare is in the stone," she affirmed.

Her Groom smiled at her recognition and told Lily to take off her ring and examine the inscription on the inside. It read, 'Diamond of Distress.' An intimate look passed between them. In a flash, Lily perceived that the cuts and sparkles in the gemstone were all a reflection of her suffering and how it now resulted in such eternal glory.

The royal pair laughed in unison, rejoicing in the wisdom of God. Gleaming walls made of pure, precious stones so wondrously set, caused Lily to stare in awe. The River of Life flowed peacefully through the Garden of Freedom that they had just re-entered through magnificent open gates on which were perched two white macaws with golden tails and wings. They flapped their wings with excitement and said, "Hail your Majesties!"

Carlotta and Favour whose face and hands Lily could now see, stood at attention at either side of the entrance while his faithful two companions stood facing the couple further in. Loving and Kindness held a token of their appreciation in their mouths. This was a sash made out of their ribbons bearing their names printed in silver and gold in the middle.

The white stallion stopped and greeted them and then turned his head around and said, "Lily, they want you to have this as a reward for completing your journey."

Lily looked gratefully at the two generous animals and said, "Thank you both very much."

Favour approached with a gracious bow and asked, "May I adorn you?"

Lily looked into his kind, light-grey eyes and responded, "With pleasure!" as he lifted up the sash and placed it over her shoulder.

"I am so honoured!" she cried and Favour smiled at them both and went to pat his companions who had moved to the side. The couple rode on waving goodbye.

A spectacular, central fountain applauded the arrival of bride and Groom. Next, a winsome white mare came into view, patiently waiting in the garden. The horse neighed in celebration as they passed by and followed them.

"That's yours," Lily was informed.

"Mine!" she said in blissful awe.

Her Groom nodded as they moved up another stunning, beautiful garden path that led to the Palace. Lily's heart quivered with joy. He dismounted and tenderly lifted her in His strong, protective arms. Lily's horse came towards her and introduced itself.

"I am your humble servant, White Wonder."

She stroked the horse's mouth with a smile and traced one of the tiny gold bells it wore around its neck with her finger and then returned her gaze to her Lord's face. White Wonder went to stand beside the Groom's horse.

The wedded couple started to ascend the steps that led to the Palace entrance. He was taking her into the place prepared for her in His Father's house, to receive her unto Himself, as He had promised.

He took her into a special room that she instantly recognised. As she entered the room, the attendant fell face down before her.

"Woe is me!" he groaned.

Lily looked into her Groom's eyes then bent down and gently touched the attendant on his shoulder and he immediately gained strength to stand before her.

"Stuart, all is forgiven," Lily compassionately stated and the attendant smiled then graciously kissed her hand with gratitude.

After handing her bouquet to the attendant, who was actually the former, scornful steward, the King said to him, "I am able to keep you from falling Stuart and to present you faultless in My presence just like Lily."[74]

The Bridegroom looked lovingly at the steward and added, "I delight in honouring the humble." He then held Lily's waist and serenaded His bride:

You are the love of My heart
Lily you are the joy of My soul
I receive you with gladness
I've banished your sadness
Forever you'll dwell in shalom
My presence your glorious home.

In joyful abandon they glided over the marble floors, as glorious rays of light and angelic music filled the atmosphere. It seemed to Lily that stars were twinkling all around her.

As they sat down, Lily leaned on her Lord's bosom and said, "Your words have come true."

With a jubilant smile He replied, "Lily My love, My words will *never* pass away. I will perform all My counsel and fulfil My every promise. I cannot lie for I am the Truth and My words express Me. My promises are My dreams for you and they will all come true."[75]

His touch was so powerful, so magnetic, so endearing. His fragrance was utterly divine. Lily was intoxicated with His presence. She noticed the battle scars indelibly marked on His hands and instinctively held and kissed His hands in thanksgiving and worship.

"No one could ever take you out of My hands Lily. That's forever settled. I have another surprise for you My dear," He advised and then said, "close your eyes for just a moment."

This she did and then opened them when she was given a ruby, voile pouch tied with fine, golden cords with a red poppy at its centre. Excited and expectant, Lily quickly pulled the cords and drew out a 24ct gold medal in the shape of a sword studded with tiny rubies crossed with an axe on which the word 'Acts' was engraved in tiny silver letters.

She scrutinized the gift and then with eyes shining with appreciation responded, "It's lovely! Thank You Lord. A perfect reminder of how I have overcome with determination."[76]

"Indeed!" He affirmed as He carefully pinned the medal on her gown. "It gives Me great pleasure to reward you. Your essence Lily is wholly pleasing to Me!"

He joyfully continued, "An incomparable mix of your faith, obedience and adoration, I simply cannot resist. I confer on you now the role and title 'Guardian of the Promise.' Embrace it, keep it before your eyes, walk worthy of it and advocate it, all with grace and truth!"

Looking deeper into her eyes He said, "Come and dine," and then He raised her up off the wine-coloured, jewel-encrusted loveseat and led her through a multicoloured corridor. Lily felt like she was walking through a rainbow.

On reaching a gold double door that led to the dining room, the bride found herself surrounded by a bevy of beautiful maidens robed in solid, vibrant colours. They were her former dancing friends and they collectively held out a majestic, embroidered cape lined with gold they had sewn as she passed through the corridor.

The King delighted in the skilful work of His handmaidens and after gracing Lily with this splendid garment, invited them all into the dining room. Inside Lily beheld a wedding feast fit for a king and with great joy she affirmed, "He has brought me to the banqueting house and His banner over me is love!"[77]

Lily surveyed the room which was excellently furnished with gold and solid oak decorative chairs and tables that seemed to have no end. A great sea of people was seated before her. Beautiful gold, fuschia and royal purple tasselled curtains draped the windows. The glory of the Lord lit up the immense room, filling it with His awesome presence. The gold and royal blue patterned deep pile carpet was heavenly to walk on. But nothing compared to the reality of heaven than her Bridegroom Himself revealed.

Trumpets sounded as they entered the room and the seated guests stood up and declared, "The King's daughter is all glorious within: her clothing is of wrought gold. She shall be brought to the King in robes of many colours; the virgins her companions who follow her, shall be brought to You. With gladness and rejoicing they shall be brought. They shall enter the King's palace."[78]

Lily was overjoyed as she greeted the guests. They had used another entrance to this elaborate dining hall and surprised her. She hadn't left the Church at all. How could she? She was part of it - the glorious corporate body of Christ.[79]

To the right near the balcony was assembled the royal harmonic orchestra, conducted by the noble Vinnel, permeating the air with an unforgettable, timeless anthem. In the left corner was a plethora of presents from floor to ceiling in all shapes and sizes smartly displayed as a wedding tree.

Marcus stood next to it, dressed in a gold bow tie and beside him was a beautiful, crafted, wooden box with the words 'Hearts of the Covenant' engraved in gold on the front, in which the wedding cards were placed. He smiled at Lily and said, "Destination reached!"

Lily nodded and remarked, "These cards express just that, thank you Marcus!" and she kissed him on the brow.

The most succulent fruit, freshly made bread and other mouth-watering edibles filled the exquisitely garnished tables. Floral blooms formed an intricate runner on each table and prominently placed was a three tiered sponge wedding cake embellished with berries. Golden-topped bottles of wine dotted the display and her bridal bouquet was set in an elegant, crystal vase at the centre of the chief table.

Lily turned to the Perfumer standing near her, lightly squeezed her hand and remarked, "I'm overcome with delight, I can hardly take it all in. Thank you so much Perfumer, you're the best maid of honour one could hope for. You look stunning as usual."

"You are welcome and worth it Lily; your compliment is gratifying."

A beautiful framed picture hung on the far wall to her left. It portrayed the moment she had shown Ron the cube in the marquis. The words 'best portion' were displayed. She scanned the room and found the two brothers who nodded as she mouthed her thanks.

After taking their seats, the Bridegroom lifted Lily's hand and stood up. The room then fell quiet. He magnanimously declared, "As is the royal custom, I have saved the best for last."

A round of applause followed His announcement and the stewards advanced to the tables. Stuart served the head table and dexterously uncorked a wine bottle and began pouring the sparkling contents into Lily's glass.

The Bridegroom held high His filled glass and joyfully pronounced, "I am grateful to see you all here. It is My Father's good pleasure to have a full house."[80]

A transparent glorious light filled the room and the Father declared, "Welcome My beloved children to the Marriage Supper of the Lamb! Share in Our mutual joy and delight yourselves in My firstborn, who is preeminent in all things!"

Jesus continued, "I have spent My life to this end - to see the preparations and invitations We have made culminate in this grand occasion. *Each* of you has a special place in My kingdom. Thank you for accepting and participating in the royal proposal. To see the fruit of My labour is more rewarding than I can describe. Eat, O friends, drink, yes drink deeply My beloved ones!"[81]

The great assembly clinked their glasses and said in unison, "We will remember Your love more than wine."[82]

"Positively superb!" remarked Tajio after a refreshing sip, the connoisseur grinned from ear to ear.

Mr. Parkinson looking grand, smiled at Lily and said, "Your company is most delightful."

Then Percy caught Lily's eye and lifted his wooden flute with a knowing look. Lily took a deep breath in recognition, nodded and turned to the Carpenter beside her. As He addressed the great multitude, Lily thought that He appeared as a shepherd feeding his flock, nourishing their souls and as the Creator taking pleasure in His new creation, His bride.

He turned to look at Lily and continued, "Lily, My beautiful, beloved bride, you have captivated My heart with one look of your eyes, with one link of your necklace and your flowing tresses. Your love is better than wine. I have a wonderful future planned for us. You seal My heart with fulfilment." He ecstatically raised His glass and toasted, "To Lily!"

"To Lily!" resounded the jubilant gathering.

The sweet strains of Vinnel's oratorio resumed.

Lily took great joy in Her Lord's auspicious words and as she gazed upon His face, she lovingly confessed to her seated guests, "The King has brought me into His chambers. His mouth is most sweet. He is altogether lovely, the Chief of all men, this is my Beloved, this is my Friend."[83]

♡ ♡ ♡

Lily awoke from this amazing dream with her heart filled with song and gladness. A melody was in her spirit and she arose and lifted her voice, expressing her heart:

Lord I want You to hold me,
Let Your loving arms enfold me,
How I long to be closer to You.
Captivate my heart now,
As in Your presence I bow,
My body and my soul yield to You.
And I cry holy, holy, holy is the Lord,
And I cry lovely, lovely, lovely is the Lord.

She glanced at the clock and discovered that it was only thirty-three minutes past three in the morning! It had seemed like she was dreaming for ages. Lily wondered if time had been suspended.

Was she seeing things? Yes and no. The clock was still working, but she had been given a glimpse of God's kingdom and a parable of things to come. Exhilarated and unable to sleep, she decided to stay up for awhile.

"I'll use this time to pray," she said to herself. "God, You are simply *the best*. I revel in our friendship. I don't understand all I've just dreamed, but I can depend on You to teach Me. You are my King. I will love and follow You each day trusting You to guide me. Thank You for the Bible and Your Spirit's voice inside me. Your plans for Your children are so great."

Lily continued communing until nearly five o'clock, when she drifted peacefully into sleep.

♡ ♡ ♡

A week had passed since Lily experienced this wonderful dream. She had phoned Mrs. Hopkins and shared the occurrence with her. Knowing the immense import of records, Mrs. Hopkins advised her to write down the dream. Lily decided to use her electronic notebook to journal the adventure and provide easy editing.

As the days passed, more details came back to her mind, especially when she read or listened to the scriptures. It was clear that God had given her the dream as an answer to her prayer and a sign that He wanted her to live by faith in Him and His word. Not all dreams were remarkable, but this one definitely was.

'My journey proved that courage, faith, love and a selfless, winning spirit cannot be overthrown,' Lily wrote in her journal.

Her attempts to contact Charity had proven unsuccessful. Lily received no reply to her calls, messages and emails. Her visits to Charity's home only resulted in a response from Mrs. Scarlett that her daughter was unavailable.

Lily filled her days with Bible reading and research, prayer, jogging and attending meetings, some at Holy Cross. The minister, Reverend Watson, was overjoyed to hear of Lily's commitment to Christ and advised her of another good church closer to Manor Views.

She was beginning to cultivate new relationships there and found the fellowship caring, strengthening and enjoyable. A few of her friends and acquaintances from high school regularly attended and provided a fun, social network.

Never had she dreamed in her earlier days that life could be such a divine delight. The Creator of the universe was her *best* friend and eternal Father! She couldn't ask for more than that, she thought.

In her flat, lively songs of praise and encouragement could be heard from a new CD Lily had acquired. She had visited the Lion and Lamb bookstore and discovered a great selection of worship music, books and gift items. Lily also purchased a newly released CD as a surprise thank-you gift for Mrs. Hopkins, having greatly benefited from the items given to her prior to Mrs. Hopkins' departure.

Priscilla, an acquaintance from church, former student of Lincoln High and new jogging partner, had loaned Lily a workout video, which she had the thrill of playing whenever she exercised at home. Lily was just about to turn off the CD and insert the video when the post arrived. There was a letter from the university, a phone bill, a bank statement and a card from Italy.

Opening the card, she grinned with delight as the picture under the *Thinking of You* caption, was of a similar coloured butterfly that she had seen in her dream. Inside was a verse Mrs. Hopkins wanted to share.

'The sufferings of this present time cannot compare with the glory which shall be revealed in us.'[84]

"Well, isn't that the truth," Lily said with a smile.

A postcard showing the Anfiteatro Romano was enclosed. Mrs. Hopkins was eager to hear how Lily was enjoying her life in Christ and hardly mentioned her archaeological activities. Her postal and email addresses were highlighted in yellow as another indicator to Lily to contact her as soon as possible.

They had spoken for hours previously on the phone, but Mrs. Hopkins had mentioned that she would be out on sites and rarely in the office. At the bottom of her note she closed with a last minute proposal. A temporary vacancy had arisen for a student aide to assist in collating data and Mrs. Hopkins wondered if Lily would like to come and join her for a month, all expenses paid.

"This could jolly well be a divine appointment," Lily reckoned with intrigue as she stared at the ancient stones. "I wonder what keys we could unearth there."

She had been averse to flying before, but yearned to travel. She felt more secure now, knowing *whose* hands she was really in. With a sparkle in her eye she confidently declared, "Whether I'm in the air, water or on land, with Christ in me, *His* righteousness my identity and my heart pursuing Him, I can be sure that *all* things are well with my soul."

A refreshing breeze gently fingered the fronds of the fern by the open window and blew across the room as a ray of sunshine streamed through. Lily glanced at the plaque on the wall which she had recently purchased. It stated,

Now thanks be to God who always leads us in triumph in Christ, and through us diffuses the fragrance of His knowledge in every place. 2 Corinthians 2:14.

Reaching for her notebook, she sat down on the sofa with quiet contentment and prepared to send her reply.

Song to the Bride

How can you doubt that I want you?
How can you doubt My love?
How can you doubt My mercy?
What were you thinking of?
Don't you see My scars?
Won't you mark them well?
They all testify
That I paid for your eternity
That's why I chose to die.

I'd rather die than live without you
I'd rather take your punishment
I'd rather face My Father's anger
Than for you to hell be sent.

How can you doubt that I want you?
How can you doubt My love?
How can you doubt My mercy?
What were you thinking of?
Don't you read My word?
Listen to My voice?
Hear My Spirit testify
That I paid for your eternity
That's why I chose to die.

I'd rather die than live without you
I'd rather take your punishment
I'd rather face My Father's anger
Than for you to hell be sent.
So come to Me right now in prayer
I'll dry your tears, drive away your fear;

I'll wrap you in My love and make you see
That I will always want you to be with Me.

They looked unto Him and were radiant and their faces were not ashamed.
Psalm 34:5

Victor's Song

I'm moving on not looking behind me
I'm pressing ahead, by God's Spirit I'm led
I'm leaving what's been done before
I'm reaching for the open door of God's grace.

Too long I've been distracted by the pressures of the day
Too long I've been reminded of the sins of yesterday
I've got a course to finish, a goal set for my life
I'm pressing forward, not looking back like Lot's wife.

I step into His mercy, where forgiveness freely flows
I'm strengthened for the journey to face the highs and lows
Victoriously, I'm moving on.

Lily
        ♡ ♡ ♡
Loved Immensely Like You

As the bridegroom rejoices over the bride, so shall your God rejoice over you. Isaiah 62:5b

Epilogue

In every heart there is a yearning for companionship, intimacy and completeness. As Lily discovered, human love at best is imperfect, at worst self-serving and cannot fully satisfy this desire. Only God can. He put the longing there and He alone can fulfil it. That's why Jesus came and why He's coming again. He has declared, "I have come that they may have life, and that they may have it *more abundantly.*"[85]

True love never fails, but provides an *unshakeable assurance* that you can and will fulfil your destiny. You can be certain to succeed - if you trust in this love who is God. He promises a meaningful, significant life now and a happily ever after that is no fairytale, but an eternal, unbreakable covenant with those who heed His call. So press on and finish well.

Notes

Chapter 1
1. Song of Solomon 5:2
2. Psalm 34:18; 46:1
3. Romans 8:28
Chapter 2
4. Song of Solomon 5:9
5. Revelation 4:11 KJV
6. 2 Corinthians 5:8
7. John 14:6; Romans 5:8-10
8. Isaiah 64:6; 1 Samuel 16:7
9. John 3:36
10. Luke 24:45
Chapter 3
11. Song of Solomon 3:1
12. John 14:2
13. Ephesians 1:5,6; Hebrews 13:5
14. Genesis 1:3
15. John 19:30
16. Psalm 132:13-16
Chapter 4
17. Song of Solomon 1:4
18. 2 Corinthians 5:7
19. Romans 8:1
20. Isaiah 1:18,19
21. Romans 8:2; Isaiah 53:5
22. Acts 10:34 KJV
Chapter 5
23. Song of Solomon 8:7
Chapter 6
24. Song of Solomon 2:2
25. Philippians 1:21, 3:7,8
26. Isaiah 59:2
Chapter 7
27. Song of Solomon 6:11 AMP
28. Proverbs 31:30 KJV
29. Matthew 16:26
30. Psalm 119:11; 1 Cor. 10:13
Chapter 8
31. Song of Solomon 4:6
32. Isaiah 54:17
33. Proverbs 3:5
34. Psalm 119:105
35. Proverbs 3:6

Chapter 9
36. Song of Solomon 8:5
37. Joshua 1:9; Matthew 11:28
38. Hebrews 10:38
39. Acts 20:35
40. Psalm 34:18
41. Psalm 34:19
42. 2 Corinthians 12:9
43. Matthew 22:12,13
44. John 20:29
45. Isaiah 54:17b; Psalm 138:8
46. Ephesians 5:27
47. Hebrews 12:29
48. Proverbs 23:21
49. Esther 1:12; Luke 17:32
50. Romans 8:31 (paraphrase)
51. Philippians 3:13,14
52. Song of Solomon 7:10
53. Revelation 3:18
54. Revelation 16:15
55. Matthew 19:26
56. Song of Solomon 2:10
57. 1 Peter 5:5; Philippians 3:10
    2 Timothy 2:12; Hebrews 12:2
58. John 8:32
59. Ephesians 4:14
60. Galatians 6:7; Hebrews 11:6
61. Isaiah 54:10; Romans 8:28
62. Song of Solomon 6:10 TLB
Chapter 10
63. Song of Solomon 7:1
64. Song of Solomon 4:7
65. Song of Solomon 4:1
66. Psalm 45:11
67. Matthew 25:21
68. Revelation 21:5
69. Revelation 19:6,7 KJV
70. Joel 2:26,27
71. Isaiah 61:10
72. Song of Solomon 2:10-13 AMP
73. 2 Corinthians 5:17
74. Jude 24
75. Matthew 24:35; Isaiah 44:26
76. Revelation 12:11
77. Song of Solomon 2:4
78. Psalm 45:13-15
79. Ephesians 1:22,23
80. Luke 14:23

81. Song of Solomon 5:1b
82. Song of Solomon 1:4b
83. Song of Solomon 5:10,16
84. Romans 8:18
Epilogue
85. John 10:10b

www.ingramcontent.com/pod-product-compliance
Lightning Source LLC
Chambersburg PA
CBHW072003170626
46813CB00005B/1998